MIDNIGHT MASS

SIERRA SIMONE

This is a work of fiction. References to real people, places,
organizations, events, and products are intended to
provide a sense of authenticity and are used fictitiously.
All characters, incidents, and dialogue are drawn from the
author's imagination and not to be construed as real.

Cover by Emily Wittig 2022
Interior formatting by Caitlin Greer

To all the lambs out there.
Thank you for being part of this journey.

PROLOGUE

Sometimes I think I'm haunted by the ghosts of my former selves.

There's the small boy who used to run into his sister's room after having a nightmare. There's the teenager who pulled that same sister from a rafter in his parents' garage. There's the college student who drowned his pain in aggressive sex and whiskey.

And then there's the parish priest who couldn't stop himself from falling in love.

I feel them crowding behind me as I walk across Princeton's tree-filled campus. I hear them whispering as I make love to my wife.

I see them behind my eyelids when I kneel to pray.

Of all the ghosts that haunt me, it is the priest who stays the closest, who dogs my steps from dawn until dusk. It's the priest who reminds me of my sins, of everything I've left behind, of every part of secular life that is flat and colorless and petty.

It is the priest who tells me to be afraid of being punished.

Like I'm not already afraid.

But I never expected my punishment to come so soon.

CHAPTER ONE

Moonlight poured into the room like a diaphanous waterfall, thick and pooling on the floor. I'd been staring at that moonlight for an hour now, trying to fall asleep, but sleep refused to come. Instead, my brain kept running through arguments against theological theism and rifling through remembered Aquinas quotes.

The danger of being mid-dissertation, I supposed.

I rolled over to be closer to Poppy, my wife and my lamb, who was currently fast asleep and facing away from me, her knees drawn up to her chest. I ran a hand over the swell of her hip, the lace of her boy shorts tickling my palm and pulling my mind slowly but steadily away from long-dead Catholic philosophers.

I moved closer to her, pressing my lips to the back of her neck and curling my body around hers. She was warm. Soft. Lavender-scented.

Mine.

Even after three years of marriage, that word still punctured me, pained me with the beautiful awe and wonder of it all. This woman, this polished, driven, smart-as-fuck woman, had chosen me.

And now I was hard.

So very hard.

I wanted to wake her up. I wanted to roll her onto her back and wedge my knee between her thighs. I wanted to hook a finger in the crotch of those panties and pull them aside, and then I wanted to sink into her. I wanted to fuck her until I came, and then I wanted to fuck her again. Hell, I wanted to fuck her all night and all day until we left for her parents' Newport mansion for Thanksgiving in a couple of days.

My upcoming dissertation deadline and her busy work schedule meant that there'd been a lot of nights in the last twelve months that we'd gone without each other, and now I lived with a constant gnawing lust deep in the pit of my stomach—a hunger that never felt completely sated, even immediately after we had sex. Poppy teased me about the feast or famine nature of our sex life this year, and I hoped that the teasing didn't mask a deeper unhappiness. Because I knew I was certainly unhappy about it.

And it was my dissertation causing it. So in a way, it was my fault, which made me even more unhappy. But this project was the culmination of the last four years of my study, the pinnacle of this new, post-clergy phase of my life. It was fascinating and meaningful and magical, and those long, silent nights in my library stall were so peaceful and rewarding. I was finally in the dusty, scholarly cave I'd wanted to be in for so long. Just…why did it have to come at the expense of time with Poppy?

Tonight had been prototypical of our new life. She'd sent me a text in the afternoon:

Come home early tonight. I am excited to tell you about my day!

So I'd promised Poppy I'd be home from the library in time to eat a late dinner. And then dinnertime came and went, and so I promised her I'd be home before ten. And then I found an annotated set of Paul Tillich's essays in the Barth collection and lost track of time, and when I finally checked the clock, it was past two a.m. I'd rushed home, racing past Trinity Church, jogging with my heavy laptop bag the whole way to our townhouse—a narrow brick thing close to the cemetery. When I walked into the bedroom, I saw a sight that was now heartbreakingly familiar to me: Poppy in her adorable lace sleeper set, asleep with the light on and her finger in between the pages of a mystery novel, as if she'd closed it thinking she would rest her eyes for just a minute.

She'd tried to wait up for me, like she always did. And I'd failed her.

Like I always did.

I'd shrugged off my laptop bag and sank onto the bed, not even trying to quash the self-recriminating bitterness that squeezed my heart and repeated all the things I already knew.

You don't deserve her.

You'll never deserve her.

And the worst: *You failed at being a priest. Now you'll fail at being a husband.*

It didn't matter that the dissertation was almost done. It didn't matter that I'd blocked off all of Thanksgiving break to be with her, and that by Christmas, I would have unlimited time and attention to shower upon her.

What mattered was that she waited up for me, night after night, like a princess in a tower. And unlike the fairytale princes, I never rode to her rescue.

And so now here I was curled against her, with a throbbing erection and a guilty heart, and how could I wake her up to fuck her this late when she'd waited all night, alone, for me? What kind of selfish jackass would I be if I did that?

With a mental groan, I rolled onto my back, my dick screaming obscenities at me as it left the warm, firm cradle of her ass. It was more instinct than intention when my hand found my cock, though I couldn't say the same for my other hand, which gently palmed her ass again.

I should go to the shower, I thought. But somehow that felt more shameful than simply jacking off here, and honestly, I wanted her more than I wanted my release. I wanted to be close to her, feeling her, and if I couldn't have that, then I would rather wait until morning.

Except…shit. She'd have to work early tomorrow, since she'd be taking the rest of the week off. And she'd probably work late too, and I had a five o'clock meeting with my dissertation advisor, which meant I'd be taken by The Revision Frenzy afterwards.

This might be the most I got until it was time to drive to Rhode Island. And if she was waking up early, it would be doubly shitty of me to rouse her now just to satisfy my needs.

I pumped my cock a few times, glancing down and then allowing myself another silent groan as I dropped my head back and let go of myself.

Just sleep it off, Tyler. You're a big boy, you can go without an orgasm for a day.

Even if it had actually been four days, fourteen hours and thirty-seven minutes, but who was counting? I had gone without sex for three years once.

Marriage had spoiled me, apparently.

I was naked and even the feeling of the sheet against me was too much, so I pulled the sheet down, laid back and tried to let the cool air in the room do the necessary work and put my body—especially certain parts of it—to sleep.

And that's when Poppy decided to wake up.

I felt her stretch beside me, her legs extending out as she

slowly turned onto her back. Through the sheet, I could see the supple muscles of her dancer's thighs, the slope of her waist and hips. Under her sheer lace tank top, her nipples hardened as the sheet slipped down to her stomach.

My grand plan to sleep off my erection was not off to a great start, not with the world's sexiest woman stretching and squirming sleepily next to me.

Her hazel eyes fluttered open, the moon's rays painting them a pale green and amber.

"Tyler?" she murmured, voice sleep-thick and huskier than normal.

"Lamb," I whispered. *She has to be up in about two hours; I should tell her to go back to sleep.*

I should I should I should.

She blinked and yawned, her lips a sweet shell pink without their trademark red lipstick. Her lips stayed slightly parted after she yawned; her lips were almost always parted because her two front teeth were slightly too big, and the effect was that her mouth always looked open and ready.

And then her eyes were a little clearer, her expression more alert. She propped her head up on her hand, moving closer to me.

"What time did you get home?"

"About an hour ago."

A little frown chased across her lips, and I couldn't tell if it was unhappiness because of the toll she thinks all this work is taking on me or if she was simply unhappy. But the frown vanished the moment she caught sight of my cock, hard and dusky and ridged with veins.

Looking at her looking at my cock was enough to make it swell and bob, now much too hard to lie flat against my abs.

She licked her lips. I didn't bother to keep my next groan silent.

"Don't make me ask you," she warned, and I knew exactly what she meant. She didn't want to ask for me to handle her the way she liked to be handled. She didn't want to beg for my dominant side to be uncaged.

Not tonight, the subtext to her request said. *Not when I need to be reminded that things are still okay.*

The thing was that I needed to be reminded that things were okay, too.

I looked her in the eyes. "Say 'red' if it gets to be too much. If you can't speak, pinch my thigh. Understood?"

The moment she nodded, my hand was laced in her dark chestnut hair and I was dragging her to my groin.

"Suck me," I commanded, shoving her head down as my other hand held my cock upright. The minute her lips grazed my tip, I hissed, losing all control and thrusting up into her warm, wet mouth before she was completely ready. And shit, it was so perfect, so wet, and her tongue was doing the most incredible things. I could easily climax just by lying back and letting her service me. And while that idea was appealing, I decided tonight called for something different.

Something a little more aggressive.

I grabbed her hair again, yanking her head up and pulling her aside as I climbed off the bed, and then I forced her to lay flat on her back with her head hanging over the edge. I was standing up now, and our bed was the perfect height to—*yes*—fuck her mouth. Fascinated, I watched the delicate workings of her throat as my cock pressed in past her lips, past her tongue, and all the way in. I cupped a hand over her neck as I pulled out and pushed back in, feeling the thrust of my cock through her skin.

The next time I slid inside her throat, she swallowed against me, her throat squeezing the head of my dick and her tongue pressing hard against my shaft and her lips sealing tightly around my base.

"Jesus," I muttered, and then she swallowed against me again, and I had to make a hasty retreat from her mouth to make sure I could keep going.

Fuck, that had felt good. Sinfully, amazingly good.

And still I wanted more. Her cunt. Her ass. Every tight, wet part of her. I wanted to claim her, over and over again.

I tugged impatiently at her tank top, exposing her pert little tits, the perfect size for my hand to cup. I didn't cup them now, though, just thumbed the furled nipples while I resumed fucking her mouth, giving each breast a sharp slap once in a while. I saw her hand snaking down her stomach, and I didn't stop her, watching as she began playing with her clit.

"Good lamb," I told her. "Rub that pussy for me."

She moaned around my dick, the vibration going straight through me, reverberating up my spine.

"Now use one finger to trace around your hole." She obeyed, and when she did, all the breath left my body, like I'd been punched in the stomach. "Yeah, just like that, baby."

Somehow, the angle made the scene all the more tantalizing: how I couldn't quite see her cunt, just the swell of her mound and the glistening of her wet finger as it circled into view and disappeared again. How I could hear the faintly wet noise of her touching her pussy.

I gave her nipple a gentle pluck. "Now push inside. Two fingers."

She moaned again, and even over the moan, I could hear the delicious sound of her slowly fucking herself. "Good girl," I ordered. "Harder now. Faster."

I pulled out of her mouth and stared at the show in front of me—her tits jiggling as she fingered her pussy, her boy shorts shoved to one side just like I'd fantasized about doing myself not moments ago—all while she tongued and sucked on my balls.

"I wish you could see how filthy you look right now," I told her. "I can't decide whether I should make a filthy girl like you come on her own fingers…or come on my cock."

Her mouth pulled away, enough for her to murmur, "Please," her lips tickling my sensitive skin.

"Please what, lamb? Let you come? Fuck you? No, don't stop with your fingers yet. Keep going."

Her hips lifted off the bed, her breathing growing shallow and uneven. She was close. "I want you," she managed.

And I wanted her. So badly. "If you make yourself come, then you can have me. How about that?"

I felt her nod, and then within seconds, she was gasping through her climax. I watched it all greedily, unable to wait for her to come down before I was sitting on the bed, pulling her on top of my cock, groaning into her tits as I impaled her on me in one, savage move.

She cried out, burying her face in my neck, and there was nothing in my world but clouds of silky, lavender-smelling hair and the feel of her firm ass in my hands, and her pussy wet and sweet on my dick.

I moved her on me, not up and down, but back and forth, the way she liked, making sure that her clit ground against the flat muscle above my cock every time she moved. "God, you're so fucking beautiful," I murmured, holding her close as we rocked. "So fucking gorgeous."

Thank you, I told God as Poppy's body began trembling over mine. *Thank you so much.*

Is it weird to pray during sex? Maybe it is, but sometimes it happens. I've tried to accept that it's who I am—a man who loves God, and who loves fucking, that I can be dirty and holy all in the same moment.

Poppy's head fell back as her second orgasm took her, and I bit at her exposed throat and breasts as she panted and shuddered and clawed at my back. This time I let her feel every wave and every flutter while I was inside of her, stretching her and filling her.

And when she finally, *finally*, stilled, warm and limp and sated, I eased her off and onto the bed.

This next part was for her.

I took her hand and wrapped it around my cock, which was now so hard that it *hurt*, dark and rigid in the moonlight. It stood straight up from my groin, the flared cap swollen and darker than the rest, and beaded with pre-cum.

The minute her fingers closed over me, I lost the ability to think or to breathe. It was only deep emotional memory that forced me to stay still, sitting on the edge of the bed, my feet flat on the floor and one hand braced behind me. I used my other hand to cradle hers, guiding her strokes, feeling the Poppy-wet skin of my erection sliding with her hand.

I had to stay still so she could see it. Because as responsive and needy as my lamb was, there was one thing in the world that turned her on more than anything else, and it was the sight of me coming. The actual act of it—my sounds, my expressions, and most of all, my dick pulsing in her hand or cunt or mouth or *wherever*, and then spilling its seed.

When she traveled, that was what she wanted to see

when we Skyped. When I commanded her to touch herself, that was the mental image that pushed her over the edge. And the few times of the year that I let her take control and make me her slave—that was where her games always led.

I didn't like to disappoint my lamb. Especially when I'd disappointed her in other ways.

Her grip tightened as her eyes raked from my face down to my tensing stomach down to where she was jerking me off, and she used her other hand to trace the furrows of my abs, the line of dark hair that ran from my navel to my groin.

Her face was hungry and she bit her lip as her hand worked faster and faster, and I felt four days worth of deprivation coiling deep in my core.

"So good," I said raggedly. "You jack me off so good, lamb."

Her lips grazed my ear as she leaned closer. "Come for me, Father Bell."

Jesus Christ.

My balls seized, my stomach clenched—every muscle in my abdomen flexing—as I uncontrollably fucked her fist—and my fist around hers—tighter and harder and faster until I was cursing—

Fuck

Fuck

Fuck

—Because she hardly ever called me that and it shouldn't be hot, it shouldn't make me come. But the moment she uttered those breathy words, I was a man possessed, thrusting up between our joined fingers until I came in huge, milky spurts, coming and coming, and spilling over our hands and jetting onto my chest and her arm and still it kept coming, and before I was even finished, she was pushing me flat on my back and licking me clean. My dick, my abs, my navel, my hand. Even the delicate spot behind my balls, her tongue was there, laving off every drop of my climax.

And by the time she was done, I was fucking hard again.

"Hands and knees," I ordered her, voice hoarse.

She scrambled to obey.

An hour later, we stepped out of the shower, mostly sated and bleary-eyed with the need for sleep. She wandered into our closet for a fresh pair of panties while I fell into bed, mind blissfully free of tomorrow and my imminent advisory meeting.

Poppy's phone buzzed on her end table. A short buzz— a text.

It was four in the morning. Who the fuck would text at this hour?

Buzz.

Buzz.

Buzz buzz buzz.

baleful glare. I sat up and reached for her phone. My plan mostly involved throwing it across the room, but I paused when I saw the name on the screen.

Anton Rees.

I couldn't help myself; I glanced through the texts that were on her screen. Since her phone was locked, I only saw the first line of each and they all seemed innocuous enough:

Just landed at JFK—

London went well, call me when—

Don't forget Sophia's proposal today—

I'll be in early—

Normal co-worker stuff. If your co-worker is the vice chair of the board for your rapidly expanding, award-winning non-profit foundation.

With what I considered saintly restraint, I set the phone back down on the end table without snooping any further. I knew Poppy's phone password, but that wasn't the point. The point was that no matter how handsome and intelligent Anton Rees was, no matter how much he was passionate about the *exact same things* as my wife, no matter how many times they traveled together, I trusted her.

Once, I'd made the mistake of not trusting. When I found Poppy kissing her ex-boyfriend, I'd assumed the worst and left the scene without even trying to talk to her. She'd done it as a purposeful attempt to drive us apart, unable to bear the guilt of being the catalyst for my schism from the clergy. If I had trusted her, if I had stayed, we could have had another year together. Instead, I'd run away, believing that she was unfaithful, and we'd spent a year miserably apart.

Since then, I'd been scrupulous in my trust. Hell, I was even sort of friends with her ex-boyfriend now.

But I'd be lying if I said that Anton didn't test that.

Poppy wandered back in from the closet, clad in a red thong and nothing more, despite the chilly, drafty room.

"Anton texted you," I said, my eyes on the pebbled skin of her breasts. "Kind of late to be texting, don't you think?"

"It's actually early, you night owl," she teased as she crawled back into bed. Without any hesitation, she snuggled her body into mine, so that my chest pressed against her back and our legs were slotted together. "He flew in from London this morning. He'll probably go straight to the office."

"Mm." It was a noncommittal noise. A Tyler-trying-to-be-an-understanding-husband noise.

Normally, Poppy would call me on it. She would turn in my arms and search my eyes and lasso the truth out of me. One of my favorite things about Poppy is that she forced me to open up and be honest about my own needs. After years of being a counselor and a resource for other people, it was gratifying to have someone do the same for me.

But not tonight. Tonight, she laced her hands through mine and sighed. "Do you still want to have children?"

Well, that was an abrupt change of subject.

"Of course I do," I said, kissing the back of her neck. "I want you to be pregnant all the time. I want you to have nine thousand of my babies."

She giggled, and I pressed my hands against her stomach, smiling into her neck. I loved her laugh. It sounded noble, royal even, like I was the knight who'd managed to charm his way into some queen's bed.

"Nine thousand is a tall order, even for us," she said.

"Nine hundred?"

"Still a bit ambitious."

"Okay," I sighed heavily. "Nine, then. You did it, you talked me down."

"Nine kids." She tried to keep a flat, mock-serious tone, but she failed, dissolving into sleep-delirious giggles again.

"I'm Irish, Poppy. Genetically we can have no less than nine children."

"Or what? Saint Patrick will chase all the snakes back into Ireland?"

"How did you know? We only tell that to initiates into the ritual."

"Is the ritual drinking whiskey and singing 'Molly Malone'? You forget that I've spent the last three Saint Patrick's Days with your family."

I chafed a hand along her goose bump-riddled arm and then reached down for the quilt folded at the side of the bed. "Ah, my sweet WASP-y bride. So much to learn."

"As long as I get to learn it with you," she said sleepily,

and my heart panged because *fuck* I loved her so much. And *double-fuck*, she would only get another hour to sleep before she'd have to get up for work.

I spread the quilt over us both, curled my body around hers once more, and by the time I got resettled, she was snoring softly, fast asleep.

CHAPTER
TWO

"And your tux is being delivered this afternoon, so don't forget to bring it inside," Poppy was saying.

I sat up, rubbing my eyes and yawning. It was still dark, but Poppy's heels clicked across the hardwood floor as she leaned down to give me a quick kiss. Even in the dark I could see her red lipstick.

I grabbed her elbows as she came closer, pulling her onto my lap. "C'mere," I said sleepily.

"I have to go," she protested faintly, but my hand was already between her legs, slipping past that red thong.

"Mmm-hmm?"

"I'm going to be late and…*Oh*. Mmm."

My fingers were inside her now, probing gently. "You were saying about my tux?" I asked huskily, feeling her getting slippery for me.

"It's for the gala on Saturday," she breathed. "For the

opening of the flagship studio. Want you…*oh*. Oh my God."

"I know you want me," I assured her, pushing her thong farther to the side and then hiking up her dress.

"I mean—want you there. Means a lot to me."

Her voice had changed, and I looked up at her, meeting her gaze in the low light spilling in from the bathroom. "Please, Tyler. I want you by my side at the gala. I've worked so hard and I want you there to see it and tell me you're proud of me."

Her voice was almost shy as she admitted it, and through my sleep and lust-filled fog, my chest squeezed. "Of course, lamb. I'll be there. And you do know that I'm proud of you, right? Of everything you've done with The Danforth Studio?"

She bit her lip and nodded, and I took that opportunity to rock my groin against her. "I'm also so fucking proud of this pussy. I want to tell everyone I know about it. I want it on the front page of every society paper."

She laughed, but the laughing turned to moans as I finally sank inside of her, and those moans turned to cries, and my poor wife ended up being late to work.

I cultivate guilt the way a farmer cultivates land.

Long furrows of regret here, heaped mounds of shame there. I weed away the excuses and the rationalizations, I water the sprouts of self-loathing with more self-loathing, I harvest it all and store it away—silos of contrition and self-condemnation and the knowledge I can't ever atone for all the things I've done wrong.

The sister I didn't save.

The vocation I abandoned.

The wife I'm neglecting.

Of course, I know—cerebrally—that life isn't atonement. That sin and redemption aren't an exchange economy where you can pay x amount of guilt or service or sacrifice for y amount of sin.

But it sure feels that way sometimes.

I read somewhere that shame and guilt activate the reward centers in your brain, that indulging in these negative feelings actually gives your brain a small dopamine-fueled boost. And maybe that's all my guilt amounts to—an almost instinctive prodding of my limbic system, an addict unscrewing the cap on another swig because I can't help myself.

But I've lived with my guilt so long, I don't know how to let it go.

I don't know if I want to.

All of this stormed and circled in my mind that morning as I did my usual Tuesday morning routine. I went to the gym for a couple hours, drowning out my thoughts with loud music and sweat. And then I drove down to Trenton to help out a local soup kitchen, bundling hygiene items and sorting through old clothes.

And then I called Millie around lunchtime, like I did every Tuesday. Millie had been my first friend when I moved to Weston to become a priest, and she had also been one of my most stalwart allies as I left the priesthood. It had almost been more difficult to leave her than my own family when I moved to New England.

"Tyler," she croaked when she answered the phone. "How are you, my boy?"

Drowning in this stupid dissertation. Worried about alienating my wife. Unsure what happens after I get this degree. "Busy," I answered neutrally as I guided my truck onto I-295.

"Don't lie to me," she chided. "I hear all your thoughts in that voice of yours. You never were any good at hiding your feelings."

No, I supposed I wasn't.

"How's Pinewoods Village?" I asked, changing the subject so we didn't have to talk about the hurricane of stress that was my life right now.

"Terrible," she complained. "It's full of old people here."

I couldn't help but smile at that. Millie had just turned ninety-two years old and still considered herself apart from "those geezers," as she often called them. She'd lived independently (and very actively) in Weston, Missouri until just last year, when a vicious bout with pneumonia and a broken hip made it impossible to live on her own. Her children had decided to move her to a nursing home in

Kansas City, and after a life being the woman who got shit done—first in her job as one of the first female engineers hired by the state of Missouri—and then later in her church and her community, Millie now had to let people do things for her. Personal things, like helping her brush her hair or tie her shoes.

She was frustrated and miserable and I couldn't blame her. I would be, too. Which made me all the more determined not to unload my problems on her.

As if she could sense what I was thinking, she said, "You might as well tell me, Tyler. Please. It will distract me from this place. They keep trying to feed me *prune juice*. Do you know how many years I've managed not to drink that stuff?"

I snorted. "I suppose they won't let you add some gin to that juice?"

"The Baptists run this place and they're fucking teetotalers," the ninety-two year old woman said. "Now tell me what's going on."

I flicked on my wipers as a light drizzle began to fall. "It's really nothing, Millie. My dissertation defense is ten days away, and once that's over, everything will be good again."

"So you admit it's not good now?"

I sighed. "I didn't say that."

"You might as well have. What is it? Too much studying? Is The Danforth Studio taking too much of Poppy's time?"

24

"Both," I admitted. "It's both. And Poppy hasn't said anything about how busy I am, but I feel so guilty…"

"But you love the research and writing, right?"

"Of course I do. I love it so much, which is why this is so hard. And she loves The Danforth Studio and all the work she's doing. Still…I can't help but feel like we're slipping away from each other."

Millie took a minute to answer. "Has she done anything to make you feel that way? Or are you just inventing doom?"

I almost sputtered at that. "I don't *invent doom*—"

"My dear boy, you most certainly do. Look back and really think—is there anything she's said or done to indicate she's angry with you? Or frustrated with your absence? Or are you simply projecting your own guilt onto her?"

I hit my turn signal as I crossed lanes to get to the exit ramp for Princeton. "Well. When you put it that way, I guess…maybe I have been letting my guilt take the reins there."

She coughed—a wet, hacking noise that made the back of my neck prickle. It was the kind of cough that meant hospitals and doctors and tests. It was the kind of cough that, at Millie's age, couldn't be ignored.

"Are you feeling okay?" I asked quietly. I didn't want to contribute to her feeling infirm or helpless, but at the same time, I worried about her. She was part of my family now, as close to my mother and my brothers as either of my grandmothers had been when they were alive. And suddenly, I felt very, very aware of the geographical distance between us.

"I'm fine," she said after she finished her coughing fit. She was trying to hide it, but I could tell she was having trouble catching her breath. "Just a little cold."

"Please tell a nurse. They can give you something."

She made a scoffing dismissive noise. "They can give me prune juice and more bedrest. And if I spend another day in bed, I will starting digging an escape tunnel with the spoon they send in with my Jell-O."

That made me laugh. "Okay, Millie. I believe you. Just feel better and have a good Thanksgiving, okay? I know Mom is planning on stopping by."

"I hope she stops by with some real food," Millie muttered. "Goodbye, Tyler."

"Goodbye, Millie."

I parked my truck in front of the townhouse, the wipers still squeaking in slow, disconsolate arcs, thinking about what Millie had said. My guilt was my language, my sustenance, my pulse. And maybe Millie was right—I was letting it bleed into parts of my life where it didn't belong.

I leaned my head against the steering wheel, not sure what to pray for. It felt wrong to pray for my guilt to disappear, just as it felt wrong to pray that Poppy would indulge this ridiculous degree of mine for just a couple weeks longer.

Help, I prayed instead. *Help me.*

Today was not a magic day. There was no well-timed song on the radio with lyrics that fit my life just so. There was no bright chink in the steel-gray clouds above me. There wasn't even that feeling I sometimes I had that at least my prayer had been heard, had been logged away in some heavenly messaging system.

Today there was just more drizzle and the eternal November cold and the whirr and squeak of the windshield wipers.

Today there was just me and my guilt, and God was nowhere to be found.

I called Poppy after the undergraduate lecture I taught and before my advisor meeting, and when she picked up, her voice was sunny and polished and breathy all at once.

"Tyler," she said, her voice half smile, half murmur. I got hard just hearing it, casually crossing my legs as I waited outside my advisor's office.

"Lamb," I murmured back, relishing the way her breathing increased, wishing I could see if a flush was creeping up her chest and neck. "I wanted to see how your day was going."

"It's been busy, but very good," she said. "Just trying to get everything together for Thanksgiving and then the gala right after that, but things have just been falling into place. People here have been supporting this whole event so much…supporting *me* so much. I really have the best staff imaginable. And the best job. And I love it. And I love you."

A glow settled somewhere in the middle of my chest. Poppy was honest and elegant and thoughtful, but she was rarely this overtly *cheery*, and hearing that husky voice I loved so much filled with happiness…well, it made me happy just to hear it. A bubble of hope floated in my mind: Millie was right, of course. I had been projecting. Poppy was fine. My marriage was fine. It would all be okay—better than okay even.

Buoyed by this thought, I teased, "You're in a good mood for only having gotten a few hours of sleep."

She laughed and I had to reach down to adjust my slacks. Fuck, that laugh got me so hot for her. "Maybe I'm in a good mood because of the reason I missed so much sleep," she teased back.

"I love hearing you like this," I said. "I love hearing you happy."

"You better get used to it," she said, a little coyly, and that glow in my chest intensified. So she realized that this trial of my PhD was almost at an end. That things would be back to the way they should be soon.

"Trust me, lamb, the minute my defense is finished, I'm dragging you off to bed and I'm not letting you leave for a month. I'm going to be yours, body and mind and soul, for as long as it takes to prove to you—"

Her laugh echoed in the earpiece again and I stopped, a

smile on my face, to ask her what she thought was so funny about my plans to make up for lost time, and then I heard muffled chattering, as if she were talking with her mouth pointed away from the phone.

And then I heard a male voice.

Anton Rees.

The smile slowly slid off my face as I listened to their indistinguishable back-and-forth, the warm and friendly cadence of their words, the earnest tone he used with her. And suddenly it occurred to me that all of the things she said about having a great staff, about having so much support—she meant Anton. Anton was there, being great and supportive, and here I was, a thirty-three year old PhD candidate with an erection in a fluorescent-lit hallway.

Jealousy stabbed at me. Stabbed and stabbed, until finally Poppy said, in that merry kind of voice that meant she'd been laughing, "Sorry, Tyler. Anton came in with some news."

"I want you this evening," I cut in, without bothering to transition from one subject to another. "I want you ass up with your hands clawing at the bed while you come around my cock."

I didn't care that only a door separated me from my advisor or that another student could walk by at any moment. I only cared about staking my claim. About showing her how *supportive* Tyler Bell could be while he gave his wife back-to-back anal orgasms.

Her breath hitched. "Jesus Christ."

"So that's a yes?"

There was a pause, a pause where I could feel her palpable want even through the phone, as if it were pulsing through whatever satellite waves made phones work. But when she answered, she was regretful. "You know I want to, but there's still so much to do for the gala…"

Rejection scraped its serrated blade along the skin of my heart. "Oh. Right. Of course."

"And you'll get me all day tomorrow and the day after that and the day after that," she added hurriedly. "And I'll be all yours then. It's just right now, Anton and I are still scrambling to lock everything into place for Saturday night."

Anton and I.

Anton and I.

"Of course, Poppy," I said again, hoping she couldn't hear how hurt and ashamed and angry I was. Not angry with her, but angry with myself. Why had I come on to her like a horny teenager, like me fucking her was the most important thing that she could possibly have on her mind? What kind of selfish prick was I?

Anton would probably never come on to her like that.

He's not coming on to her, I told myself firmly. *Every time you've met him, he's been perfectly nice. Perfectly polite. You're letting jealousy invent scenarios that aren't happening.*

Except what if those scenarios were happening?

Dammit, Tyler. Stop it.

"And I'll probably be late tonight, but I know that you'll be working late at the library anyway, so I still may get home before you." More muffled chatter, Anton again.

"Okay," I said, as evenly as I could. "I'll definitely see you tomorrow then. For our trip to your parents'."

"It's a date," she affirmed, but despite the upward inflection of her tone and the sweet goodbye she added after it, I could tell that her mind was already back on her work. Back to Anton.

"Goodbye, lamb," I said softly and pressed end.

She was right. I'd probably be working late anyway, so it didn't matter that she would be doing the same. And we'd have Thanksgiving together.

But as the student scheduled before me left my advisor's office and I stood to gather my things, I felt that small bubble of hope pop, the space where it had been filling with the leaden weight of guilt and suspicion.

CHAPTER
THREE

Papers rustled. My chair squeaked as I leaned back, trying to relax. My advisor, Professor Courtney Morales, lifted her mug and took a sip of decaffeinated coffee.

Finally she looked up. "This is strong work, Tyler. I'm very impressed."

I couldn't hide my relieved exhale, and she smiled a little, shifting in her chair with a small wince. She was in her early forties, black and beautiful with a gorgeous halo of obsidian, corkscrew curls—and also nine months pregnant. She tapped her fingers idly on the firm swell of her stomach as she looked down at the last fifty pages of my thesis.

I could see a few marks here and there—her penned-in notes and suggestions—but nothing insane. Could this mean that I wouldn't have any major revisions before my defense? Could I be…*done*?

Professor Morales flipped a few pages over, took

another sip of fake coffee, and then looked up once more. "However, I think we need to revisit your conclusion."

I pushed down the initial swell of panic. The conclusion was twenty-seven pages and had taken me almost a month to write. "When you say 'revisit'…"

"It needs to be rewritten," she said bluntly. "This is an amazing work, Tyler. I've watched it grow from an idea with raw potential into a fully rounded and layered piece. But you're robbing yourself with this conclusion."

My mouth was dry. "How so?"

"You spend almost two hundred pages systemically examining the difference between notional belief and religious practice in the Catholic Church. You deconstruct established dogma and retranslate St. Anselm's *credo ut intelligam* as a pledge of commitment rather than a forced intellectual assent to said dogma. *Yet*, your conclusion is twenty-seven pages of passive circumvention."

I suppose I must have had a very dejected expression on my face, because she shook her head with a sigh. "I can't handle those sad green eyes, Tyler. I'm not saying it's poorly written; the prose, as always, is excellent and the logic is precise. On the surface, it's impeccable. But it's not what this work needs."

I was almost afraid to ask. "And what does it need?"

"A call to action. You just spent a year exposing the weaknesses of the Catholic Church on a theological level, while simultaneously cataloging the things it does well.

Synthesize those things into a coherent response. Into a vision for what the Church could be. Explicitly show us how your thoughts can be worked into practical action. And then I guarantee you'll have a paper that will blow the board away."

So. I had ten days to rewrite from scratch something that had originally taken me thirty. I had a wife who was currently laughing her throaty laugh—a laugh that should belong to me, *dammit*—with Fucking Anton. And the coffee kiosk near the library closed early, so it was just me and a half-empty room-temperature bottle of Dr. Pepper in my dim library stall, tucked away back in the stacks.

I had books piled around me, papers and highlighters scattered on every available space, multicolored Post-It flags sticking out of every book like flat neon fingers. And a laptop, with a blank Word document open, the cursor blinking accusatorially at me.

A call to action...

It was easier said than done. When my paper had just been about the academic—the dry examination of history and theology—it had felt removed from real life. It had felt safe.

But writing about ways that the Catholic Church should change? To become healthier and more modern? That felt very, very unsafe.

I wanted Poppy right now. I wanted her hands on my

shoulders as she rubbed my anxiety away. I wanted to feel her solid, graceful faith in the divine and in me as we prayed together. I wanted to hide from this mess with her—fucking or drinking or cuddling or just listening to her amazingly articulate voice as she told me about her day.

But Poppy was busy (with Stupid Fucking Anton), and so I called the next best thing.

Father Jordan.

Jordan Brady was maybe my best friend, although I wasn't sure if I was his. His best friend was most likely a dead saint that probably visited him in his dreams or some shit, and it was hard to compete with a dead saint. Still, though, we were close, and he'd seen me through some of the worst parts of my life. He had the most genuine faith of anyone I'd ever met, and if anyone had a direct line to God, it was him. And if anyone could help steer me through this, he could.

The phone rang a few times before he picked up, and when he did, I recognized the slightly dazed voice he sometimes had after performing Mass, as if the ancient rite had unmoored him from our time and space, and sent him drifting into another realm.

"Tyler," he said, a little dreamily. "I thought you'd call soon."

"You are so weird," I told him. (Lovingly.)

"Is this about Poppy?" he asked, ignoring me.

"No, it's about my dissertation." I explained to him

what Professor Morales wanted, and how I thought she was right, but also how daunting the rewrite felt. "Especially because I feel like I'm also criticizing people like you and Bishop Bove," I finished. "When I have nothing but the greatest respect for both of you. But it doesn't matter, right? I mean, no one reads these things except for board members. I could write anything, and it won't affect a soul outside of Princeton."

Jordan took a long time to answer, and when he did, he sounded as if he were relaying a message rather than speaking his own mind. "It's your task to write this, no matter how frightening it may seem. You should not be afraid to be critical, so long as you're seeking authentic spiritual practice. And I think many people outside of Princeton are going to read this. This will have an impact crater, Tyler."

"Thanks," I mumbled. "That's very helpful."

"Take a break," Jordan suggested. "Sleep tonight and pray, and when you wake up, things will be clearer."

I stared at my laptop for another thirty minutes after I ended my call with Jordan. And then I finally took his advice and gave up, slamming my laptop closed and shoving the piles of paper into my bag. I left the books on my desk since I could lock up my stall for the night, and then, after one last look around, I went home.

It was after eleven, and the miserable drizzle had morphed into a miserable sleet. I walked the four blocks home, shivering and despondent, trying not to think about how shitty the next ten days would be as I attempted to construct something coherent and thoughtful in a third of the time that it had taken me to write the first version.

Shit.

All I wanted to do was go home and kick off my shoes and crawl into my warm soft bed, with my warm soft lamb. The thought of her—of her smell and her petite frame and of the red lipstick that she maybe hadn't wiped off yet—hastened my steps. I'd get home, find my wife, and get warm again. Forget about this shitty dissertation and this massive, unexpected complication.

But when I unlocked the door to the townhouse, I was greeted by silent darkness. No faint reading light from the bedroom, no running water in the shower. The kitchen and living room were exactly as I'd left them before I went to teach. Poppy hadn't been home yet.

This shouldn't have bothered me. She said she was working late; hell, even I knew that she needed to work late. I knew how important this gala was to her. And yet a selfish, terrible part of me wanted her here, now, because I needed her. I was upset and frustrated, and she was my anchor. She was my harbor. She was every metaphor, nautical or otherwise, that made life worth living.

And she wasn't here for me tonight.

But as soon as I thought that, I hated myself, thinking about all the nights she'd waited up for me. She'd been here for me every other night. No, I needed to realize that her work was as high a priority for her as my dissertation was for me, and it would be good for me to get a taste of my own medicine, so to speak. I'd earned this loneliness, this sense of abandonment. It was my penance.

I graded a few papers, took a long shower and then crawled into my empty bed, closing my eyes against the silent darkness. I was sure I wouldn't be able to sleep like this, with my impending revision pounding against the inside of my skull and my skin prickling with the unpleasant awareness of the vacant space next to me.

Poppy had traveled before, yes. And there had been a few times when I'd flown home without her, sleeping alone in my twin bed from high school. But for some reason, it felt different tonight. It felt deliberate or hurtful or maybe neither of those two, but something like those. And the end result was me growing less and less tired, and more and more frustrated, until finally I got out of bed, tearing off the covers in one violent motion.

I made myself an Irish coffee—adding a bit more than the traditional splash of whiskey—and sat at our high-top kitchen table while I slowly set out my dissertation papers on my laptop.

The window by the table looked out onto the cemetery, the stones sedate and stately and ancient in the cold moonlight. The sleet had ended and the occasional snowflake spitted by, coming from the hazy, thin clouds stretched across the moon. I could see the faint glaze of ice on the blades of grass and along the tops of the grave markers. Somewhere out there, Aaron Burr and Grover Cleveland slept, famous men who were now no more than bones and ice and fragments of ragged clothing.

They didn't have dissertation conclusions to rewrite, lucky bastards.

I turned back to my laptop, flexing my fingers and started typing.

One way the Catholic Church could transform within this framework...

Backspace backspace backspace.

The Church already has many kernels of these seemingly modern conceptions...

Delete delete delete.

Tyler Bell, the priest who deserted his post, has no fucking right to talk about what the Catholic Church should or shouldn't do.

There. That was better. Professor Morales would surely accept that as a conclusion, right?

With a sigh, I turned back to the body of my dissertation, even though I could practically recite the entire thing from heart by now, trying to figure out what to say. And how to say it authentically. But all of my words seemed to blend together in the same meaningless drabble, blurs of what seemed now to me to be obvious and quotidian observations. Was it too late to run away? To take Poppy and disappear somewhere where the dissertation panel couldn't find me?

I'm not sure when I fell asleep. It happened sometime after the third Irish coffee but before dawn. When the scratch of a key in the doorknob woke me up. I had a partial imprint of the laptop keyboard on my cheek and a large yellow highlighter stain on my pajama pants from where the hand holding it had fallen off the table and into my lap.

I chafed at my face, trying to rub away the feeling of the keyboard, and only gradually did I become aware of another sound besides the usual key and purse shuffling and unlocking noises.

A man's voice.

"Thank you so much for the ride home," Poppy was calling as the doorknob turned. And then that fucking laugh—the laugh that should belong to me—she was giving him her low, rich laugh again as she told him goodbye.

I was on my feet in an instant, walking to her, walking to the door, because as much as I was trying not to be jealous, to be Understanding and Calm Tyler, having Anton Rees with my wife at my doorstep at five in the morning was a little much.

Who was I kidding? It was a lot much, and I wanted to know why it was happening.

But the door opened, and Poppy glided in, and there was only the tail end of the blue McLaren as it pulled away from our house. I hated that my eyes immediately slid over to my truck, I hated that I immediately calculated the cost difference between our cars. I hated that I wondered if Poppy had calculated it too.

I could be a worldly man sometimes, I could be a sinful man almost all the time, but materialism was not among my sins. Jealousy, yes—lust, certainly—but never greed. And so it was an uncomfortable feeling now, wishing I made more money, wishing that I could offer Poppy more than what an ex-holy man, now student could offer, which was next to nothing. As opposed to Anton, who came from the same world that Poppy did, who drove the kinds of cars and wore the kinds of suits she'd grown up surrounded by.

Poppy was smiling as she walked in, humming as she set down her purse and shrugged off her cherry-red wool coat. But then she saw me and her smile faded.

"Tyler? I didn't think you'd still be up."

I tried out a smile but it felt strange on my face, so I stopped. "I fell asleep at the table. I only woke up when you got home."

"I'm sorry," she said, turning to hang up her coat in the entryway. "We were just working so late and then late turned into early, and Anton offered to drive me home rather than me taking the train…Oh."

When she'd turned, I had been right behind her, so she turned right into my bare chest. And now I leaned forward and ran the tip of my nose along her jaw, feeling her shiver under my touch.

Is she shivering because she's turned on? Or because she has something to hide?

I was too tired to tell my brain to shut the fuck up. Instead, my jealous masculine instincts took over and I inhaled the scent of her skin. Lavender and coffee—no trace of cologne, no trace of alcohol or cigarette smoke. She hadn't touched another man, they hadn't gone out to a bar or anything similar.

She was telling the truth.

This should make me feel better. This should remind me that my tendency towards jealousy would, in Millie's words, invent doom where there was none.

But I pushed the reminder aside, picked up my wife and carried her to bed, determined to wipe away whatever supportive, friendly, McLaren-driving Anton had done with her tonight at work. Determined to bury the jealousy with every thrust and push of my cock into her pussy.

And when morning came, that sultry laugh would only belong to me.

CHAPTER FOUR

The drive to Newport was brutal. Sleet and intermittent snow turned I-95 into a miserable crawl of traffic, a slow-moving river of honking and merging and near-accidents. After Stamford, it opened up a little, but not a lot, and Poppy fell asleep listening to my audiobook about ancient Greek mythology. So I navigated through the drizzle and stroked her thigh as she snored softly and the narrator droned on about the fucked up familial politics of the Olympians.

Around Westerly, she roused, her hair adorably mussed and her large hazel eyes blinking away sleep. Yawning, she looked out the window. I didn't need to tell her we were almost here; she knew this part of New England as intimately as I knew the neighborhoods and fountains of Kansas City. I flipped the stereo from my audiobook to the Bluetooth audio. Blues rock, loud and raw and lo-fi, started pounding through the speakers.

"This should help you wake up, sleepyhead," I said, steering my truck onto US-1.

I couldn't see her smile, but I could feel it as she stretched in her seat. "Well,*someone* kept me awake last night."

She was talking about me, and the fact that I'd fucked her until the day finally dawned gray and wet outside our window. But for a minute—an instant really—I thought *someone* meant Anton, and white-hot anger pricked at my chest.

I swallowed it down. "We should be to your parents' in about an hour."

She nodded, reaching over to squeeze my thigh. I swore I could feel her every finger through my jeans, I swore I could feel the heat of her palm searing marks onto my skin. And with my jealousy beating its restless rhythm inside my chest, it only served to make me agitated in a very particular sort of way.

I glanced over at her, at her perfectly applied lipstick and sparkling eyes, and then said, "Unzip me."

She licked those flawless crimson lips and complied, her hands pale in the fading light as she unbuckled herself and reached for me.

I leaned back, giving her better access to my zipper and also so I could get the view I wanted: those manicured hands on my jeans and then parting the fly and taking hold of me.

There's something incredibly hot about driving fast with a woman unzipping your pants, something powerful about having your foot heavy on the gas and your vehicle eating up the road and a beautiful face about to be buried in your lap.

She stroked me once or twice, but I didn't need it, not with her lipstick and my restless jealousy and the engine thrumming around us as I pushed the truck faster and faster. And then she gave me one of her painfully gorgeous grins, leaning down to kiss my tip, her tongue darting out to tease me.

I should have let her take her time, I should have savored each and every one of her warm breaths as she pressed those lips everywhere, from my base to my crown, but when I looked down, I saw the red lipstick marks on my cock and I couldn't hold on to my self-control, threading my hands through her hair and pushing her head down. Her lips parted and her mouth was so fucking warm, and there was suction and heat and the fluttering of that wicked tongue…

"Shit," I swore as my dick hit the back of her throat. "Holy shit."

She moaned in response, the vibration going straight to my balls, and I dug my fingers deeper in her hair as I pressed harder on the gas, thankful for the lack of traffic but also wishing that this was more public, more exposed.

"On your knees," I said. "I want to touch your ass."

She did as she was told, easing up onto her knees, never breaking in her attention to my dick, and I was able to move my hand from her hair to her ass cheeks, rucking up the skirt of her expensive dress to reveal her expensive underwear. I gave her a small spank and then squeezed. God, I loved the feel of her ass in my hand. It was so soft and firm and just so damn juicy, the kind of ass you could play with for hours and never get bored. And the way it segued into her firm, dancer's thighs, the way it led to her warm, lace-covered folds…

I rubbed her over the damp lace, making her moan again. I spanked her once, twice, three times, alternating cheeks, and then wrapped my hand around her hair, yanking her face up to mine.

I kissed her with my eyes on the road, tasting myself on her tongue, smearing her lipstick around her mouth, and then shoving her back onto my dick, practically running the truck off the road when she put her mouth on me again.

"*Fuck*, Poppy," I managed. "Just…*fuck*."

This time, after I spanked her, I found the tight rim between her cheeks and began teasing it open, pressing inside and making her squirm. I hadn't fucked her there in far too long; I made plans to fix that as soon as humanly possible. And shit, with the way her ass clamped around my finger, hot and greedy, it was hard not to justify pulling over and making *as soon as humanly possible* happen right this very minute.

She leaned farther down, so that the head of my dick was squeezed at the back of her mouth, and then she did that swallowing thing again.

"Jesus," I muttered, my head dropping back against the headrest. She did it again, and I was so close, so fucking close, with the road hissing under my tires and my foot on the gas and her ass and hips curving into her tiny waist. With her red lipstick smeared around her lips as she sucked me, with her silky, tousled head moving in my lap, with the bass and drums of the music thumping through the car.

And then I felt it, a barbed tension in my balls, and then I was holding her head down as I shot into her mouth, over and over again, vaguely aware that I was chanting my name for her,

lamb

lamb

lamb.

And then I was aware of every pulse and throb of my orgasm in her mouth, and she swallowed it all, even milking me for more after it seemed I had no more left to give.

She cupped my balls playfully as she sat up, and I growled, "Come here," and pulled her into another kiss, wishing that our trip was nothing but this—kissing and being sucked off as I drove, just loud music and smeared lipstick and damp lace.

Alas. Nothing is ever that simple.

After stopping at a gas station so I could wash my hands and Poppy could *freshen up*—which after three years of marriage I'd learned was a term for twenty minutes of unknowable fiddling and trifling in front of a mirror—we were back on the road and to her parents' house before six o'clock.

The Danforths lived right on the coast, in the kind of hundred-year-old house that looked like it should have a name. It did have a name, in fact, Pickering Farm, although there was nothing farm-like about the stately white mansion with its gables and massive chimneys and many, many windows. It had a vast green lawn that sloped down to a rocky ledge and then to the sea, and it was surrounded by the kinds of gardens that managed to look both incredibly elegant and incredibly understated at the same time. The whole place exuded money and oozed class—the kind of money and class that didn't need to proclaim itself because it was so established and comfortable.

Everything about it reminded me of my lamb. My elegant lamb, who froze in the car with her hand on the truck's door handle.

"What is it?" I asked her, my brows furrowing together.

"Nothing," she said nervously, her eyes lifted to the house in front of us. The Danforths had already decorated for Christmas, and Christmas trees sparkled from every window, accented by candles and wreaths and garlands wrapped both inside and outside the house.

I put my hand on the back of her neck. It was a possessive gesture, but it calmed her. Her breathing slowed and then she twisted herself so she could rub her face against my arm, like a cat would.

"I just don't like coming back here," she finally admitted. Her voice was small. "It feels like defeat. Like I'm still a part of their world."

Poppy had abandoned that world the minute she'd walked across the Dartmouth graduation stage to receive her MBA, going on to wait tables and eventually dance for money, seeking a more authentic life than the gilded cage she'd grown up in.

"You're not a part of their world, lamb. You're part of *my* world, you understand? You belong to me."

That seemed to soothe her. She took a deep breath and nodded. "You're right. I belong to you. This place doesn't matter."

"Tonight, after we get settled, I can show you how much it doesn't matter," I promised, and that earned me a smile.

Inside, we were assaulted by the family—Poppy's parents and her two brothers and their wives and then the host of well-groomed nieces and nephews in their flouncing dresses and bow ties. Despite Poppy's need to flee all those years ago, her family was actually very nice—polite and intelligent and charming, if occasionally a little more proper than my Midwestern ass was used to. They'd been nothing but kind to me, even with my middle-class pedigree and non-existent income. In fact, since I had been the reason she started visiting regularly again, I think they felt very warmly for me. At least as warmly as they were capable.

I made good on my promise to Poppy after we went to bed and ate her pussy for as long as she could stand it, through silent orgasm after silent orgasm, until I finally had to clap my hand over her mouth because she couldn't keep quiet anymore. And then we fell asleep in her childhood bed, a canopy bed so wide that four people could comfortably lay together and so tall that even I had to exert myself a little to climb on top. A princess's bed in a princess's room, and the princess herself nestled in my arms, her dark hair spilling over the pillows and my arms like a sleek curtain.

The morning dawned even colder than the last, bringing with it real snow, the kind that blew more than it fell, sending forlorn gusts of wind to rattle against the windows and doors. I woke after my wife, as usual, finding her sitting at her vanity with her hair already in loose gleaming curls and her lips already bright red.

"Who's the sleepy one now?" she asked, eyebrow arched, as she fastened an earring into her earlobe. She was looking at me in the mirror as I got out of bed and walked over to her, stopping to raise my arms over my head and stretch. She stared at my reflection with undisguised fascination, staring particularly at the way my loose pajama pants slid even lower down my hips as I stretched, exposing a line of dark hair and highlighting the morning wood I was sporting.

"Come back to bed," I said in a lazy, husky voice.

She turned, fastening her other earring and standing up. "Believe me, there's nothing I would rather do. But as I recall, *you* were the one who wanted to spend Thanksgiving with my family. *You* were the one who sermonized me about the importance of family and connection. And it's Thanksgiving morning, which means Grandmamma's cinnamon rolls, and I know you don't want to miss your chance to eat some."

I opened my mouth to speak, but she held up a hand. "And yes, I know what you're about to say, and yes, I know there's something else you'd rather eat." She leaned close to whisper in my ear. "But cinnamon rolls only stay good for the eating for a handful of minutes. I'm always good for it."

She reached into my pajama pants, gave my hopeful cock a few teasing pumps, and landed a soft, light kiss on my cheek. And then her nude heels were clicking on the floor and she was gone.

She'd pay for that teasing later, I decided. In a big way. But for now, a cold shower was in order. No point in terrifying Grandmamma with my boner.

"You know, this house used to have a ballroom. But it burned down in the 1940s."

We were alone together in the massive front entry, me staring at a family portrait and Sterling coming in from the morning room. I didn't bother turning at the sound of his voice. It didn't matter how little or how much interest I showed in him, he had decided at some point four years ago that we were buddies, and there would be no shaking him.

At least I had a drink with me.

Sterling Haverford III—former trust fund kid and now a business mogul—sidled up to me with his own whiskey glass in hand, looking as smug and handsome as ever in his bespoke suit and Italian shoes. Blue eyes, black hair and cheekbones from some sort of Abercrombie and Fitch hell completed the image, and when I glanced over at him to nod an acknowledgment, I felt the familiar burn of jealousy in my chest.

Did I mention he was also Poppy's ex-boyfriend? And the man I saw her kissing the day I'd decided to leave the clergy in order to be with her?

I hated that he was handsome. I hated that he was rich. And I hated most of all that he was charming—so charming that I didn't even really hate him at all. In a weird way, he reminded me of my brothers, Sean and Aiden, who were as different from me as humanly possible, but still some of the closest people in my life. Under Sterling's veneer of money and good breeding was a horny American businessman, and with two out of three brothers meeting that definition, I knew the type pretty well.

Oblivious to my thoughts, Sterling continued, "Rumor was that my great-grandfather's uncle started the fire in the ballroom by ashing his cigar too close to an unsuspecting debutante and her giant dress."

Oh, how I loved to be reminded how historically close the Danforths and the Haverfords were. (Which was ridiculous, since Sterling and his wife being invited to share the holiday with us was reminder enough.)

"The house has recovered well," I said, moving away from the portrait and over to one of the massive Christmas trees. Surely the Danforths hired people to do these things; I couldn't imagine Margot Danforth untangling strings of lights or looping garland around a ten-foot tall tree.

"So, what's the over-under on the Cowboys stomping the Raiders this afternoon?"

Dammit. How did he always know the exact kinds of things to say to capture my attention? I fucking *loathed* the Raiders, and I tried not to miss any opportunities to explain to people why.

Which is how I found myself in the library with Sterling, both of us on our third whiskey, arguing about whether or not Roger Goodell should step down as commissioner of the NFL, and also about whether or not Margot would let us watch the game instead of playing cards. And yes, bridge is what the Danforths did after their Thanksgiving meal instead of watching football.

Blue bloods.

Sterling stood—a little unsteadily—to get me another glass of whiskey while he refilled his own. "You know, Tyler," he said as he walked to the globe bar that Mr. Danforth kept by the fireplace. "You're not half bad. And you fit in well here."

I didn't know about that. Despite the kindness of my in-laws, I still felt out of place. At home in Kansas City, Thanksgiving was fried turkey and football, naps stretched out on the carpet punctuated with games of Monopoly and Chinese checkers. Here at Pickering Farm, it was a formal coursed meal with paired wines and different forks, followed by interminable bridge games and (if we were lucky) a frigid walk along the shore. I still felt like Nick Carraway in The Great Gatsby when I was here: a passive observer at best, a charity case at worst. I wasn't family. I wasn't a Danforth or a Haverford or any other name that could be traced back to the *Mayflower* or any of the original colonies. My pedigree dissipated less than five generations back, an illegible scribble on a forgotten ledger, people who epitomized the poor, huddling masses, people who carried nothing with them across the Atlantic except for rosaries and exhaustion and hope.

I would always be a guest here.

A clumsy outsider.

A tourist in a life I could never hope to have for myself.

I accepted the glass Sterling offered, taking another warm sip before I answered. "I suppose. The Danforths have always been very nice to me."

"They like you." Sterling sat, automatically unbuttoning his jacket as he did. "Hell, I like you."

"I like you, too. Even though I think you're an asshole."

He choked on his whiskey laughing and I had to smile. It fucking pained me to admit it, but he was a hard bastard not to like. Which reminded me of how much I had detested him when we'd first met. He'd tried to blackmail me, he'd tried to steal Poppy away from me, he'd been despicable in every way…he tested my ability to forgive and think God-like, compassionate thoughts about my fellow humans.

And yet, here we were four years later, sharing whiskey and football facts. And even though I did feel that low-level jealousy every now and again, it was mostly absent from our interactions now. Somehow, I'd mastered my envy of him, and more than that, I'd come to terms with my envy of his place in Poppy's world. I would never be him, I would never be Tom or Gatsby, I'd always be Nick. I would always look out of place inside my in-law's house, just as Sterling looked perfectly at home here.

And that was okay.

"Sterling?" came a musical voice from the door. It was Penelope, his wife, looking a little desperate. I didn't blame her, given that Poppy had once considered Penelope to be her mortal enemy. It was probably difficult to find common ground with a history like that, and Sterling and I had basically abandoned the rest of the house in order to get drunk and talk about the NFL.

Sterling grumbled something unintelligible but still pushed to his feet to go to his wife. I, however, sat in the library and chewed over this new realization, this epiphany over something that had happened so gradually I hadn't even noticed it.

But if I truly wasn't jealous of Sterling any longer, how come Anton Rees made me so fucking furious? If I'd found the way to shut off that instinctive, terrible part of myself with one man who'd been interested in my lamb, why couldn't I do it with another?

CHAPTER FIVE

Thanksgiving dinner at Pickering Farm was a massive affair. More than thirty guests sat in the window-lined dining room while piano music drifted in from somewhere in the house.

Poppy seemed listless the entire meal, pushing food around her plate and not eating, even refusing dessert and wine. She made half-hearted conversation with her parents' friends and attempted a smile or two, but otherwise she continued to look tired and out of sorts. I circled my hand around the middle of her back, pressing into the sensitive spot between her shoulder blades, enjoying the feeling of her body melting into my touch.

Penelope, I thought. It must have been those two hours Sterling and I hid in the library talking guy stuff, and I'd left her (essentially) alone with a woman she abhorred.

Guilt chafed at me. What had I been thinking, leaving

her alone like that? So I could be with Sterling of all people? And now she was probably socially exhausted and emotionally drained, and I hadn't done anything to help her.

I leaned in close, my lips grazing the shell of her ear as I spoke. "Are you okay, lamb?"

She looked down at the table, as if she were avoiding eye contact with me. But then I realized it was probably Penelope and Sterling she didn't want to look at right now. "Just tired," she said quietly.

"Do you want to go lay down?"

She shook her head. "I'm fine, really." But she wasn't fine; a lone tear escaped out of the corner of her eye, trailing down her cheek as a single, clear droplet. I caught it with my thumb and pressed the thumb automatically to my mouth. It wasn't conscious or intentional, but the way Poppy's eyes followed my movement with avid interest—the first spark of life I'd seen all night—sent a rush of blood to my groin.

I knew what I wanted to do. I still had to get her back for this morning, after all, and her family was sitting at the other end of the table…

I reached under the long tablecloth and found one smooth thigh, crossed over the other, and I slowly pushed those thighs apart, all while keeping my eyes trained on Poppy's. She resisted at first, but the moment I mouthed lamb at her, her legs parted.

Maybe I didn't know what was wrong with her. Maybe

I wouldn't be able to help her even if I did. But I could do this, right here and right now, reminding her of all the things we'd promised each other and God in that church three years ago. That we loved each other. That we belonged to one another. That our love would be eternal and all-consuming, patient and kind and would not boast or envy…

Okay, so I still had work to do with the envy part. But everything else, I could demonstrate to her in the way that we communicated best: with our bodies.

Keeping my upper body still and my expression neutral, I slid my hand higher, past the pleated skirt of her Saint Laurent dress and to her warm center. She took in a deep breath, her eyes flashing, and I paused, giving her a quirked smile with a raised eyebrow.

Do you want me to stop? I asked her with that eyebrow.

In response, she spread her legs farther apart.

At the other end of the table, a vibrant conversation about an upcoming tennis match had broken out, and at our end, the non-family guests were engrossed in some foreign-property-acquisition-gone-wrong tale.

Nobody was watching us.

I ran a middle finger over the damp silk covering her cunt, knowing without needing to look that she wore a pair of panties I'd bought for her just last month, for the express reason that I liked the way the fabric felt against my fingertips. And—yes—there was the little bow at the top and the lace trim around her legs…and all of my slow, gentle exploring was taking its toll on her. She squirmed in her chair, trying to subtly rock her pelvis against my hand, spreading her legs far enough apart that I could easily skate my fingers underneath the fabric at the crotch, which I did next.

She sucked in a breath through her teeth, which no one seemed to notice, and I casually used my left hand to take a sip of wine while my right hand eased her panties off to the side and started stroking the soft skin underneath. She was wet, wet enough that there was no resistance as I circled her entrance with my middle finger. Wet enough that I could easily slide my finger up to her clit, making everything slippery and slick and effortless. The pad of my finger rubbed over her swollen bud while my thumb traced soothing circles on the bare waxed skin of her mound.

"So, Tyler," one of the guests said, angling his head to me. "Tell us more about Princeton these days. I'm a Yale man myself, but I have to admit, their Bendheim Center is doing some pretty impressive things."

Poppy flushed pink and tried to shift away from my touch, but I kept rubbing her while I leaned my other forearm on the table and turned toward the man who'd spoken.

"The Bendheim is excellent," I answered conversationally. "I honestly think they'll be adding more programs beyond a master's soon. The demand for finance and business education is simply too high to ignore."

"Princeton doesn't care about demand," another man said, in that half bluster, half chortle that these kind of men got after three or four glasses of wine. "They only care about academia."

I shrugged, using the movement to disguise the shift in my arm and shoulder so that I could—*oh fuck there it was*—press one finger slowly inside her pussy. Her ragged breath was surely undetectable to anyone but me; it was their loss, because it was the loveliest sound in the world, lovelier than the piano still playing softly, lovelier than the sound of the sea-whipped wind against the glass.

Just feeling her turned my semi into a full erection, which was thick and long and fairly uncomfortable in my narrow, low-waisted slacks. But I relished the discomfort, the feeling of being hard for her while she was so wet for me, and her held helplessly captive by my hand alone.

I pushed farther in, wiggling it a little, as the men started arguing about what Princeton's lack of a proper business school meant about its place in the Ivy League. Her hand came up and gripped the edge of the table as I finally pressed up against her G-spot, pushing against it and then dragging my finger out again to rub against her clit in hard and fast circles, then plunging back in to toy with her G-spot again.

Those perfectly imperfect front teeth dug into her lower lip so hard that I thought she might bite through it, and her knuckles were white as she held on to the table, all while I chatted casually about Princeton politics and tossed a few

Harvard jibes out there, much to the amusement of the tipsy faux-aristocrats.

"And Poppy, are you still a Dartmouth girl through and through? Even with a Princeton husband?"

She swallowed, those teeth letting up on her lip for just a second, long enough for her to manage a weak, "Still a Dartmouth girl, Richard."

I loved every millisecond of this, of my proper wife in her proper home surrounded by all these proper people, while I slowly finger-fucked her under the table. All these people talking about Ivy League colleges and investment plans and the increasing costs of yacht maintenance while the daughter of the house had her pussy stroked in the very same room.

Her head was bowed now, one hand clenching the table and the other wrapped tightly around her water glass, her cheeks pink and her breathing fast, her dress revealing the erect buds of her nipples. If anyone was paying close enough attention—which they weren't, thankfully—they'd see that something unusual was happening to her. They'd see the subtle tilt of her torso as her body overrode her mind and tried to get my fingers deeper, faster, harder.

I was so fucking hard that I thought my dick would drill a hole right through my pants, but I didn't care. I only cared about her, about owning her with just these small movements of my fingers and wrist, about making whatever had caused that tear vanish, about replacing it with pleasure.

And, if I admitted it to myself, there was something appealing about making her come only a handful of seats away from the same bastard that took her virginity. Something addictive about bringing this well-heeled young woman to the brink right in the middle of this American shrine to wealth and influence. *Who is Nick Fucking Carraway now?* I wanted to shout. *Now who doesn't belong?*

Just as I parried some man's joke about the Princeton rowing team with a riposte about Harvard's, I felt it. The tell-tale tightening in her core, that abrupt clenching, and then she was closing her eyes as I shoved two fingers inside for her to ride out her climax on. Silently, she rocked against my fingers, eyes squeezed shut and teeth buried in her lower lip. And I bit my own lip, because it was so wet down there and I could feel every pulse and quiver, every single ripple of her coming, and that drove me fucking crazy.

So fucking crazy.

I wanted to pull her onto my lap and then I wanted her to bounce on my dick until she came again. Or maybe I'd be happy with her on her knees in between my legs, sucking me off like she'd done in the truck yesterday. Or, honestly, even a quick hand job through my slacks. At this point, my dick was not too interested in the particulars.

But instead I laughed and nodded with the other people at the table while Poppy ground out the last of her orgasm, and then when she finished, I gently withdrew my fingers, pulling her panties back into place and smoothing her skirt over her legs. And when the coast was clear, I lifted my fingers to my mouth and licked her taste off of them.

Her eyes widened, but so did a shy, creeping smile, and I sat back, satisfied that I'd cheered her up, even if it was at the cost of a raging erection that had no hope of being tended to any time soon.

"What are your plans, Tyler?" one of the anonymous wives asked right as I'd finished licking my fingers. I struggled to remember her name, but honestly, they all looked the same—carefully coiffed, subtly Botox-ed, expensive brooches pinned to their wool dresses. "After you finish your doctorate? Will you teach?"

Just like that, my satisfied mood vanished, replaced by something much more ambiguous. Something much more anxious.

"I'm not sure yet," I said delicately. "I'm still focused on finishing my dissertation, so I haven't given too much thought to what comes after."

I could feel Poppy's eyes boring into the side of my face, but I didn't turn to look at her. What happened after this degree was something we didn't talk about, the proverbial elephant in the room. Poppy would want me to do something *big* and *meaningful* and *authentic*, and other words that people like her and Jordan threw around like parade confetti. To them, those words were fluttering and light, easy to grab out of the air and hold onto.

Not for me.

For so long, I'd built meaning around this one singular goal—working to make sure what happened to my sister didn't happen to anyone else. Systemic change. Institutional reform. Large scale awareness and activism.

And then came Poppy. And then came seven months digging wells and building schools in Pokot. And I started to see how seemingly small things, ordinary things, kisses and pick-up games of soccer and shoveling dirt, could be important and fulfilling.

So I didn't know what meaningful and authentic looked like for me anymore. I'd given up trying to know God's plan for my life, but I hadn't given up trying to live a *godly* life, and I wasn't sure what that meant in my new context. Did I stay in academia and guide other people in their discoveries? Did I go back to mission work? Did I find a non-clergy role in a church, maybe in administration or as a youth director?

The hard, cold truth: the only job I felt suited for—the only job I felt *made* for—was being a priest.

And I could never be one again.

The thought sent a bolt of fear through me. An electric current of panic and agitation. What if leaving the priesthood had damned me in this life as well as the next? What if I never found another calling, another vocation, and I was doomed to live my life in this perpetual state of restlessness, searching for an answer that I would never find?

"That's too bad," the anonymous wife said. She was giving me one of those *why don't you come help me with my tennis swing* smiles that all these wives seemed to give me when I was here. "You have so much to give the world."

Then came the men, now completely drunk, offering me jobs and referrals, and then the hired waiters cleared dessert off the table and it was time for cards. I frowned at my wine glass while my plate was taken away, my stomach churning, fucking miserable with myself and my future and this Gatsby house and my life.

"Tyler," Poppy said quietly, touching my arm. I looked around; we were the only ones left at the table. In my brooding, I hadn't noticed everyone adjourning to the next room.

We stood, and I took the opportunity to quickly adjust my lingering erection. I followed Poppy as she walked around the table, her dress hugging the slender dip of her waist and flouncing over her pert ass, the hem hitting the middle of those toned and creamy thighs…

I took her arm and yanked her into the corridor, pulling her into the small room off the foyer that served as the coatroom, closing the door behind us. The only light in here was a weak golden glow from the Christmas trees in the foyer, seeping in from under the door.

"What are you—"

I put a hand over her mouth as I spun her around so that she faced away from me. I was upset and I was angry with that stupid question from the dining room, the question that forced me to confront yet another part of my life I was failing at, and Poppy was so beautiful and soft and *mine*, and I was still so fucking hard for her.

I nudged her feet apart as I flipped her skirt over her ass. I didn't care that this was her parents' house or that anybody could walk in here to get their coat or purse. I only cared about the sharp intake of breath she gave as I pulled her silk underwear down her legs and stuffed them in my pocket.

"Say red if you have to, lamb. Otherwise, keep that pretty mouth shut."

She shuddered at my words, at my hand checking to see if her cunt was ready for me, at my other hand flat on her back and pressing her forward. She braced her hands against the wall and looked back over her shoulder, kohl-rimmed eyes smoldering at me.

Fuck, she was hot.

I unbuckled my belt with one hand and then unzipped my pants, loving the way she unconsciously arched herself closer when she heard the purr of my zipper.

I stepped even closer to her, grabbing my cock and lining it up with her entrance. I paused though, right before I shoved inside, wondering if this was an immoral thing to do. To use the woman I loved as a salve for yet another of my spiritual dilemmas. To use her body and those willing hazel eyes for a few minutes of respite from my guilt and anxiety.

But then she took the decision away from me, pressing her ass into my hips and impaling herself on my shaft.

My lips parted as my erection slid home, and I swore I could feel every single millimeter of her cunt as it swallowed my dick, every fucking one. For a minute, I just stood there, absorbing the feeling. She felt so wet and so tight, so *good*, and in the faint light I could see the outline of her bent over, the heart shape of her ass pressed into my groin.

I grabbed her hip with one hand and her upper arm with the other, bringing her upright and closer to me, and even with her heels on, I had to bend my knees for my petite lamb. But I knew the second I found the perfect angle, because she let out a low, breathy moan, and then I began to thrust in earnest, deep, curved thrusts that made her hands reach back to dig into my thighs.

Silence was of the essence, but I couldn't help but to fuck her hard. The kind of hard where the slap of our skin and the wetness of our fucking and the smack of my balls against her cunt made distinct noises that not even these repressed New Englanders could fail to identify.

I didn't care. Because for a few minutes, life was perfect again. My lamb and I, alone, fused as one. No family, no ex-boyfriends, no looming future. No dissertations and no Anton. Just us, and the jagged sighs of my wife as I found her clit—still sensitive from the dining room finger-fucking—and teased it. It didn't take long, thirty seconds maybe, and then her stomach muscles clenched and her pussy squeezed around me.

She shoved her fist into her mouth to keep from crying out, and then everything released, powerful contractions that milked my own orgasm from me. I leaned over her back and bit her shoulder as I pumped my cum into her, deep inside her sweet body.

I felt the climax everywhere—the muscles of my thighs and abs, my spine, my toes. Every part of me released into her and she welcomed me, all of me, the messy heat of my insatiable lust and the unbearable weight of my guilt and the uncertainty ahead of us. Somehow she took it, and for the first time in weeks, my mind felt quiet. My heart felt at peace.

I pulled out, wiping us both dry with her panties. They went back into my pocket, and I helped her straighten her dress while she buckled my belt.

In the dim gold light, I could barely see her face tilted up to mine, those blinking eyes, those entrancing lips. "Is everything okay?" she asked. "You seemed…preoccupied."

"Is that your way of asking why I dragged you into a coat closet to fuck you?"

Her throaty, queenly laugh. "Yes."

"I'm fine now," I said honestly. "You healed me."

"With my magical vagina?" she asked skeptically.

"With your magical vagina," I confirmed. "And just by being you." I cupped her face with one hand, wondering if she could see my eyes as clearly as I could see hers in the dusky light. "Sometimes I don't think you know how much I love you."

She turned her face into my hand, and I brought my other hand up to trace her jaw. *She really has no idea*, I realized. How just by being *her*, royal, sexy Poppy, she made me a better man. She made me feel at peace. She made me more like myself. I worried that she only saw herself through certain lenses—the lens of her family, maybe, or her own lens, which was harsh and overly critical and unyieldingly demanding.

She never really appreciated how smart she was, or how talented. She never seemed to realize exactly how gorgeous she was and how much I craved her. To fuck, certainly, but also simply to stare at. Staring at her made me happy. I couldn't think of a simpler way to describe it than that. She was so beautiful to me that all I had to do was watch her, and life made sense again.

The first time we'd made love, she'd been my communion, a new covenant that I was making between her and me and God. I had thought that was the most intense— the most luminously spiritual and carnal—moment we could ever share, but somehow that covenant had grown, until now every time I looked at her, I felt like a convert newly baptized. I felt like the Apostles witnessing the Transfiguration.

God was my god. But Poppy…Poppy was my prophet.

I opened my mouth to tell her this, but then she pressed

a finger to my lips, her mouth lilting into a mischievous smile. "I hear someone outside," she whispered.

I did too, the clinking of ice in a glass, the droning tones of yet another WASP-y dialogue about horses and boats. We stood there, frozen, Poppy fighting off a fit of near-teenagerish giggles at almost being caught in the coat closet. When the conversation finally died away as the speakers moved into another room, we let ourselves out of the closet and scampered up to our room, where I covered my protesting prophet in kisses and herded her into the shower, where we proceeded to get clean—and then dirty—and then clean again.

CHAPTER
SIX

It wasn't until the drive home that it came.

The idea.

Poppy had again drifted off, after making me promise to help her put up the Christmas tree once we got home. Once she started snoring, I figured it was safe to turn off the Christmas music she'd put on and listen to my audiobook again.

The narrator was relating the story of Theseus and the Labyrinth of Crete, and as I thought about the labyrinth itself, I began to think of other iconic symbols in mythology. Celtic knots and crosses and triskelions and spirals. And then I thought only about spirals as I drove down the wet but mostly empty highway, and then it came to me why I struggled with jealousy over Anton, even though I'd let go of my jealousy over Sterling.

Life is a spiral.

As long as we lived, we would keep moving forward. But on a spiral path, getting closer to your destination meant periodically passing the same things—emotions, issues, character flaws—over and over again, the way a person walking up a spiral staircase would continually find himself facing north every ten steps or so.

My jealousy was my north, and perhaps I was wiser than the last time I had encountered it. Perhaps this time it would be easier to master, and then when I inevitably faced it again, it would be even easier...

But my mind didn't stop there. Because I realized that this didn't just apply to individuals. It applied to institutions too. Like churches. Like the Catholic Church, actually. Because historically, the church had its own spiral, times where it had been forced to modernize or adapt, great leaps forward in humanitarianism and philosophy, and giant leaps back with dogma and persecution.

The Church didn't need me to tell it how to change. It already knew how, because it had done it so many times before.

The Catholic Church doesn't need a prescription for reformation, I composed mentally, wishing I were at my laptop and able to type this out. *The Church only needs a call to awaken...*

Oh my God. Had I really broken through the barrier of my dissertation's conclusion? Could I finally write this motherfucker?

Excited, I sped up the truck and glanced at the clock. Only a couple hours until home. And then I would start kicking this rewrite's ass.

"I thought you said we'd put up the tree together?" Poppy said, her arms folded.

I was on my way out the door, and I'd stopped to give her an absent-minded kiss—rookie mistake. Because then she'd noticed my laptop bag stuffed full of snacks and deduced that I was planning on being gone the whole night.

I ran a hand through my hair. I hated disappointing her—Poppy loved Christmas the way most people loved babies—fiercely and sometimes irrationally—and we'd put up the tree together every year since we'd been married. On the other hand, every minute I stood here arguing with her was another minute wasted, when I could be tapping out the words that would finally bring this cursed thesis to its end.

"Can we put it up another evening?" I asked, trying to sound penitent and genuinely eager. (I was neither.)

Her lower lip bowed into something dangerously like a pout. My heart lurched at the sight, but then my brain chanted *write write, finish finish*, at me, and my heart stopped with the guilt.

"It's the day after Thanksgiving," she said. "That's the day Christmas trees are supposed to be put up, but if you want to wait…"

"I do, thank you. I promise the minute I finish this thing that we can put up seven Christmas trees, okay? We'll put up as many as your mom has at Pickering Farm." I dropped another kiss on her unmoving lips. "I'll be done with this thing so soon. I swear."

Her arms were still folded when I walked out the door.

The next afternoon, I knocked on the open door to Professor Morales's office. "Professor? Can I come in?"

Morales stood at the small window of her office, rubbing her lower back with the heel of one palm. She didn't give me an immediate response, so I just hovered at the threshold like a vampire, until she finally turned to me. Her lips made a flat, unhappy line, and her eyes were distant and murky.

"Is this a bad time?" I asked. I'd nearly jumped up and clicked my heels in the air when I'd seen her light on as I walked from my tiny shared office to the library, and I decided to take the chance to show her my latest revision. I'd spent the night at the library last night, coming home late this morning to shower and indulge in a quick nap before I drove to campus in the latest round of freezing sleet. Poppy hadn't been home—I'd assumed she'd run off early to prepare for the gala—but the Christmas tree in the living room to greet me instead, a seven-foot monument to my failures as a husband, winking away in the dim gray light of winter.

I told her we could put it up later, I'd thought irritably. Putting it up without me seemed rather passive-aggressive, and I'd let the resentment rankle in my chest as I showered and lain down to nap. I'd finally had a breakthrough, we were finally at the end game, and she was going to start doing things without me now? Now, when we were so close to the end of all this bullshit?

But I wasn't programmed for anger. I was programmed for guilt. And it wasn't long before my irritation was superseded by depressing fantasies of Poppy hanging ornaments herself, drinking eggnog by herself, singing off-key carols by herself.

By herself. Those were the two worst words in the English language right now, or at least the most incriminating.

With difficulty, I moved my mind from the Christmas tree back to the present. Morales was leaning forward now, one hand braced on her desk as she stared lock-jawed into the middle distance. And then she let out a low groan—the kind of noise that I normally heard when my wife was on her hands and knees in front of me—and so I blushed in automatic response, until I realized that Morales was in pain, real and excruciating pain, and I stepped forward to go to her.

"Professor? Would you like me to get someone?"

"I think I need to call my doctor," she managed after a minute or so. Her body relaxed slightly, but she kept leaning forward, as if afraid that standing up would trigger her pain again.

"Um, okay," I said, letting my laptop bag slide off my shoulder and digging my phone out of my blazer pocket. "What's her name? Maybe I can find her number online."

"I can do it," she said, and her voice was a little less strained now, a little more lucid. "Will you bring me my purse?"

I did so and she found her own phone, and within a few minutes, she was talking to a nurse, things like *six minutes apart* and *thought it was just back pain* and *no, no it hasn't broken.*

Which was around the time that I realized that she was in labor. Holy shit.

Holy.

Shit.

Once, I'd been qualified to baptize babies. I'd been qualified to join people together in marriage, and I'd been qualified to pray at their bedside. I'd guided people through some of the happiest and unhappiest parts of their lives, the highs and lows, the agonies and the ecstasies.

But I had no idea what the fuck to do with a woman in labor. Especially a woman who potentially held the weight of my academic future in her hands.

"Okay," she said into the phone. And then, "Yes, I have a ride to the hospital."

Like a character in a sitcom, I instinctively glanced

behind me, as if searching for another person in the room, and then I realized—*I* was the ride to the hospital.

As if sensing my burgeoning panic, Morales met my eyes as she hung up the phone. "Tyler," she said. "You have to stop with those puppy eyes. I can't handle them even when I'm not—*ugh*." She bent over again, both hands on the desk, breathing hard.

Unsure of what to do, I patted her awkwardly on the back.

"Don't. Touch. Me," she snarled.

"Yes, ma'am."

After another minute of this, she finally straightened up. "Where are you parked?"

"Outside the building in the faculty lot. Should I bring the car around or…?"

"Fuck it, we'll walk." She eased herself upright, made a flapping motion with her hand to indicate that I should grab her purse, and then started walking. I felt like a fifteen-year-old, awkward and useless. I had no idea what to say or even which hospital entrance to pull up to when we got there. Surely, I should be doing something, right? The weird breathing stuff—they always did that in the movies.

When I glimpsed her wedding ring flashing in the light of the hallway as we walked out, I asked, "Should I call Mr. Morales?"

Professor Morales shot me the same withering look she gave clueless undergrads in her medieval church history classes. "Do you honestly think I took my husband's name when I got married?"

"Um. No?"

"Hell no, I didn't. And my husband is visiting family because the baby wasn't actually due until next week…oh shit." She stopped about three feet away from the elevator, her hands extended, as if looking for something to grab onto. I offered my arm, which I instantly regretted, because she dug her fingers into me so hard I knew I'd bruise later. But I bore it up as stoically as I could, and when she gritted out a request to knead her lower back, I reached around her and did it, hoping no one walked by and saw me basically embracing one of the members of my dissertation board.

And so it went all the way down to the truck, a few minutes of walking, a few minutes of stopping and laboring, where she gradually turned all the bones in my hands into loose pebbles and I kneaded her back as hard as I could. In the truck, she faced the seat backwards and hung off the headrest while I called her husband and left him a (very awkward) voicemail explaining why I was driving his laboring wife to the hospital.

It only took me ten minutes to make a twenty-minute drive, but by the time I pulled up at the Emergency Room entrance, Professor Morales had gone from definitely in labor to abso-fucking-lutely in labor, and just the few steps from the truck to the front door took us several minutes. A nurse came out with a wheelchair, earning herself the most vicious run of curse words I'd ever heard from Morales, and when I tried to peel myself away to park the truck, I was informed in no uncertain language that I was staying the fuck with her. So I did, letting her crush my hand and swear profanities at me that would even make the Business Brothers blush, until we made it up to a room on the labor and delivery ward.

"Are you the father?" a nurse asked me.

"No," I stammered. "I'm her PhD candidate."

The nurse squinted at me like I was an insane person, and I kind of felt like one, surrounded by all these bustling nurses and monitors and then I made the mistake of looking over and seeing a nurse with her hand up Morales's—

"I'm going to go park the truck," I said uneasily, backing away. "Is there like a sister or a friend we can call to help with—" I gestured at the nurse/hand/vagina situation on the bed. "—All of this?"

There was a sister, it turned out. And then Morales's husband called back, excited as hell and racing to the airport in a taxi, and by the time I'd parked the truck, Morales knew her husband was on his way and her sister was walking into the room. I stationed myself in the waiting room, examining my arm for bruises and feeling weirdly jittery. Why was I jittery? This wasn't my baby.

But then I realized that what I thought were jitters were actually slivers of joy—bright, vibrant things piercing the fog of work and guilt. Morales was having a *baby*, right now, here in this very building. And I'd gotten to be a part of it, a part of this new life, this incredible, beautiful thing that was happening despite wars and genocides and bad politicians and shitty academic politics.

I couldn't wait until I was in the hospital for my own baby. I sat back and let myself fantasize about it, about Poppy with a swollen belly, about Poppy swearing obscenities at me. About us, growing our family. It almost became too painful to think about—Poppy having my child—not because it made me upset, but because it made me so incandescently happy. I started smiling just thinking about it, wondering if she would agree to trying for a baby as soon as I finished my degree. Hell, we could do it now, because a baby wouldn't be born for another nine months after he or she was conceived, although I should then really buckle down and think about what happens after this PhD. I couldn't ask Poppy to have my child if I didn't have a plan for my own life yet.

"Mr. Bell?" A nurse came out into the waiting room. "Ms. Morales wants you to know that she just delivered a healthy baby girl, and that you're welcome to come in and meet her."

I shouldn't intrude, I really shouldn't...

"Alright then," I said, standing and following the nurse back into the room. As I did, I glanced at the clock. It had only been two hours since we'd gotten to the hospital, which seemed fast for having a baby...not that I really knew anything about having babies. My brothers had no kids, and Poppy's brothers had their children long before I'd met her. Really, my only baby experience was from baptisms, and those tended to be fairly short affairs.

When I came into the room, Morales had fresh plum lipstick on and an expensive cardigan pulled over her hospital gown. "I'm sorry for all the things I said to you earlier, Tyler," she apologized briskly. "I'm feeling much better now."

"Yeah, now that they've given you pain medicine," her sister pointed out.

Morales nodded towards the bundle in her arms. "Would you like to meet my daughter?"

I crept towards the bed, suddenly feeling shy—a feeling Morales rid me of quickly, by stretching the little bundle out for me to hold the second I was close enough. I didn't know a lot about babies, but etiquette suggested it would be rude to refuse a proffered baby, so I accepted, surprised at how little the infant weighed.

I tucked her into the crook of my arm and peered down at her little face, her eyes slightly swollen and her head capped by a blue and pink striped hat. But she was awake and almost preternaturally calm, her dark eyes blinking and her little mouth parted, as if she were staring in wonder at the world around her. She was so unearthly, so perfect and yet so fragile, and in that moment, where her wide eyes seemed to peer up into mine, I felt both a peace and a turbulent joy, almost like giddiness.

I had heard many explanations for why Abraham had named his son Isaac, which means he laughs in Hebrew. That it was because Sarah had laughed when the Lord told her she'd bear a child, or even that he was named for God's own laughter at the situation. But right now, I knew how Abraham might have felt, holding his own newborn, a bliss so triumphant and euphoric that he couldn't help but laugh.

I kissed the little girl's forehead, my chest rending itself open with adoration and hope, and then I (reluctantly) handed her back to Morales, who gave me a tired smile. "Bet you didn't anticipate spending your Saturday night like this."

"Beats writing in the library." I smiled back, except then something cold and panicked seeped through my thoughts, like a blaring alarm that only becomes gradually discernible as you rouse yourself from sleep.

Saturday night.

There was something about Saturday night.

Out of habit, I checked my phone, where the calendar notification showed me exactly what that something was, and also that I was already an hour late to it.

Poppy's gala.

CHAPTER SEVEN

On a good day, it takes about ninety minutes to get from our townhouse to the new flagship Danforth Studio in Manhattan. And when it comes to New Jersey traffic, it's rarely a good day. So it was three hours past the gala's start time when I finally skidded into the studio, my dress shoes sliding against the smooth wood floors as I made for the event space in the open loft above the main studio room.

I'd tried calling Poppy on my way home, and then again several times on the way there, and there'd been no answer. No answer to my texts either, and that was how I knew.

She was furious with me.

But there was a baby! My mind protested, as if she were already arguing with me. *You can't be mad at a baby!*

Once she would let me explain everything, it would be fine. I was sure of it.

I just had to find her first.

The gala was still in full swing. The stars twinkled in the many large skylights above. Tipsy donors danced as a band jazzed their way through Gershwin; waiters circulated with endless rounds of drinks; people chatted and laughed on the edges of the dance floor. I searched frantically for Poppy, pushing past the guests as gently as I could, even though I felt like punching my way through the crowd. I had to find her, I had to explain why I was late, late even though she had explicitly explained to me how important it was that I support her tonight.

Shit.

I'd really fucked up this time.

I caught a glimpse of bright red lace out of the corner of my eye, and I swiveled on my heel, seeking it out. And then there she was, hair swept high off her neck, a small cross hanging in the dip of her collarbone. The dress plunged to a low, lacy neckline, showing off the uppermost curves of her perfect tits, and while the lace flounced out into a tea-length skirt, the nude-colored sheath under it stopped mid-thigh. Metallic gold heels and that emblematic crimson lipstick completed the look. For a moment, all the blood went from my brain to my dick, and my tuxedo pants became entirely too tight. I'd love to fuck her in all that lace. I'd love for her to spread those shiny heels while I knelt in front of her and lifted her skirt, and then I'd eat her pussy right where she stood.

I smoothed my jacket down and subtly adjusted myself

as I moved forward, and then I stopped. Poppy had so arrested my thoughts that I hadn't noticed whom she was standing next to. Not just standing next to—she had her arm around his waist and his arm was strung casually over her shoulders, a lingering side-hug as they laughed with a pair of donors and she gestured with her champagne glass.

Anger balled in my stomach, anger that I had no right to feel, but felt anyway. Here I was on the spiral again, except I couldn't be scholarly or enlightened about my continuing struggles with jealousy, not now. Not with Fucking Anton touching my wife so casually, so familiarly, as if they held each other like this all the time.

As I started walking again, my hands practically burning with the urge to throttle Anton, I remembered a picture from my children's bible growing up. It was an illustration of Jesus chasing the moneylenders and merchants out of the Temple courts, one hand scattering a pile of coins to the ground while the other was raised high. In that hand, he'd held a whip poised to rain brutality on the defilers who'd polluted the most sacred space in Jerusalem. There had been overturned tables and broken stools and people fleeing and scattering, and all of that sounded exactly like what I wanted right now. To be flipping tables and lashing out in anger, to drive away the bastard who was touching my wife—*my* sacred space.

Poppy turned to say something to one of the donors and then froze as she caught sight of me stalking toward her.

Several emotions flitted across her face—shock and anger and relief and worry—and then her good-breeding and expensive education whirred to life, replacing her raw expression with a controlled and elegant mask.

When I reached her, all I wanted to do was pick her up and drag her off. I wanted to toss her over my shoulder or grab her by the neck or any number of possessive actions that would show Anton—and Poppy—whom she belonged to. Who owned her.

But while all of those things were sexy and consensual in bed, they were shitty and misogynistic in public, especially at an event like this one, the culmination of years of hard work and one so full of influential donors. And I wasn't so consumed with jealousy and possession that I'd forgotten the difference between the bedroom and the outside world.

It was a close thing, though. Even as I shoved my hands into my tuxedo pockets, even as I deliberately stopped out of range to make sure I didn't cave to my urges and physically pull her away from Anton.

She's a grown woman. They're only friends. You're just being jealous.

And besides, you are the one in trouble right now.

All of that was hard to remember with Anton hugging her. I dragged my eyes away from the spot where his hand cupped her shoulder and met my wife's gaze.

"Good evening, Poppy. Anton. Sorry I'm late."

I knew, even before I finished talking, that I had not successfully scrubbed the jealousy from my words. I knew that my expression surely betrayed every conflicted emotion that I felt. All of this was confirmed when the two donors mumbled excuses, and left Poppy, Anton and me alone.

That was fine. Because now Anton looked supremely uncomfortable, dropping his arm from Poppy's shoulders and clearing his throat. "Hello, Tyler."

I studied him. He was a few years older than I was, with light brown hair and amber eyes, several inches shorter than me, and—I noticed this with terrible, selfish glee—he was a little soft in the stomach and thin in the arms, something that even his well-tailored tuxedo couldn't hide.

He didn't seem abashed or flustered, at least not in the way that someone who had done something wrong would seem abashed. His discomfort seemed to come from a place of supreme shyness. In fact, he was offering me a shy smile now, and I hated the fact that he looked so handsome while he did it.

"Anton, do you mind if I speak to Poppy for a few minutes?"

"Of course," Anton said hurriedly, already moving away from us. "See you in a bit, Poppy."

He left and the band finished their song, the loft drifting into a tide of quiet chatter. Poppy and I stared at each other for a minute, me hungry for her and her angry with me, and then finally she stepped forward, so close that her dress brushed against the fabric of my tuxedo trousers.

"I don't want to talk here," she said firmly. Her heart-shaped face was tilted up to mine, that sharp chin defiantly set, and I couldn't help it, I reached up to touch her jaw.

There it was: a flutter of the eyelashes, a small intake of breath. She was as hungry for me as I was for her.

"You're mad," I said. It wasn't a question.

"Yes. And I meant what I said—I don't want to talk about this here."

"What I want right now has nothing to do with talking."

The moment I said it, I knew it was the wrong thing to say, but I didn't fucking care. Everything felt like it was closing in on us—on me—and I couldn't breathe for the stress and loneliness and anger rolling off my lamb in hot, metallic waves. I was furious and aroused and it didn't matter that I was the one who had been late, that I was the one to let her down, I only knew that my chest felt like it would burst with all the conflicting feelings inside of it. I only knew what I needed. And right now, I needed her.

If she had been a different woman, she would have slapped me. As it was, I could see spots of color blossom high in her cheeks and the lines of her neck stiffen as the band struck up a new song.

"If you think," she said in a dangerously low voice, "that this is going to end with me fucking you, you are severely mistaken."

"Will you at least listen to me? I am sorry I'm late, but—"

"It doesn't matter," she said. "Whatever you have to say, it won't help us right now."

I pressed my lips together, not trusting myself to speak because the only words that came to mind were indignant ones. Defensive ones.

Poppy leaned closer, her chest pressing into my ribs. From any other vantage than my own, it looked like a gesture of marital affection, but they couldn't see the flare of her nostrils or the diamond-hard eyes that now glared up at me. "You are so jealous of Anton, and you know what? You should be. You should be jealous, because at the end of the day, he's the one who is consistently there for me. He's the one I tell my thoughts and fears to, and he's the one who knows—" she broke off, her eyes sliding away from mine.

I found her chin with my fingers and turned her face back to mine. "Knows what, Poppy? What could he possibly know about you that I don't?" Still holding her chin, I brought my mouth to her ear. "I know the things you think about when you're alone. I know every single fantasy you have in that pretty head of yours, and I know which words and which sights get you wet. I know what the inside of your pussy feels like and I know what the inside of your soul feels like. I know what books you fall asleep reading at night and I know which blanket is your favorite to use by the fireplace and which is your favorite to use in the recliner. I know how to make you come so hard that you forget who you are, and

I know that you are so hungry for my orgasm that you'd drop to your knees right now and let me jerk off onto your face. Right here, right now, in front of all these people. Wouldn't you?"

Her breathing was rapid now, her chest expanding and deflating against my own chest, and there wasn't a part of her that wasn't covered in goose bumps. I let go of her face and pulled away, satisfied that I'd made my point, and for a minute, I thought it had really worked. I thought I'd convinced her to let go of her anger.

I was wrong.

She stumbled back as if I'd pushed her—which I had, in a way. I'd pushed her with my words, and she looked so stung and so stimulated—all wide pupils and parted lips and flushed skin—and then the tears surfaced, large glassy tears in those hazel eyes, spilling over onto her cheeks. She turned away and pushed past the guests in the loft to go downstairs.

I watched her go, that red lace fluttering around her legs as she fled from me, and I knew I should stay put. People don't run away unless they want space, and Poppy had plenty of reason to want space from me right now, given that I'd just made her cry in front of all these influential people. Guilt held me by the back of my neck, closing my throat and twisting my gut, and I just wanted to smash something—a window or a car door or even my own bones. Even more than that, I wanted to chase after her and apologize for being such a giant prick, for being the worst husband in the world.

But Feminist Ally Tyler was telling me to respect her space and her boundaries, to accept that the rest of this discussion had to happen on her terms, and that meant not running after her and bending her over the nearest table.

Fuck.

I hated doing the right thing.

Hated it.

I lifted my eyes to the ceiling, wondering what God would want me to do. There were no bible verses for how to let your partner walk away from you when you were both mad as fuck, especially when you were both horny as fuck on top of it all. There were no bible verses for having an erection in a tuxedo or for watching your wife disappear down an open flight of stairs while the slow, jazzy strains of "S'Wonderful" echoed against the high white walls and glass ceiling.

I guess I'm on my own again, even though I'm doing the right thing and it fucking sucks. Thanks a lot.

I should go home. Poppy would have to come back eventually, and we would talk then. Except, I'd probably have to work on my dissertation all day tomorrow…and the day after that and the day after that, not even counting the classes that I would have to teach, and of course not counting the fact that Poppy would have to work herself…

Shit, I missed Missouri. I missed my entire world being focused on one building—St. Margaret's—and I missed

Poppy working from home and on her own schedule. How were we supposed to fix this when we had no time together?

It didn't matter. I should go.

I started moving through the guests, towards the back staircase, when I noticed a familiar form descending down the large front stairs to the main studio, in the same trajectory Poppy had taken.

Anton was going alone, and while part of me reasoned that he probably just wanted to check on his friend whom he'd seen visibly upset as she ran away from her own party, another part of me churned back into full-blown rage. Fuck boundaries, fuck doing the right thing. He didn't get to go after my wife. That was *my* prerogative, *my* privilege, *my* job.

I changed directions and followed him, my dress shoes loud on the steps as I descended into the studio. I couldn't see Anton or Poppy, so I drifted around the corner into the long hallway that led to the smaller studio rooms, all with their large mirrors and long barres.

Empty studio after empty studio, and then, in the very last one, I saw Poppy. She was alone (thank God), hugging herself and looking out of the window, her back to the door and me. In the mingled light from the moon and the streetlights, I could see her shoulders shake as she cried softly to herself. A lone tendril of hair had escaped from her updo, hanging in an elegant curl against her neck.

I stepped into the room, closing the door softly behind me.

She turned her head, looking back over her shoulder. She didn't speak.

"Tell me to leave, and I'll leave," I said, taking another step closer. "Tell me not to touch you, and I won't."

A tear spilled over her cheek, gliding down to her jaw. But she remained silent.

"Say red or whisper it or mouth it even—and I'll go, no questions asked. I'll get a hotel room so that you can come home without me there."

Still nothing from her. I'd halved the distance between us and I kept coming closer, determined to give her a choice. To let her know that she could say no to me at any point, and that I would leave if she did.

I finally got close enough to touch my lamb, but I didn't yet. I was so fucking hard for her, and my hands practically vibrated with the need to seize her, but I didn't.

She was still looking at me over her shoulder. Tear tracks glistened on her face, and that stray lock of hair on her neck hung so gracefully against her skin…I wanted to tug on it. I wanted to bite that neck and suck hard on the delicate skin there.

"Just say red or leave or go, at any time. And I will stop." I met her eyes. "Do you understand?"

Without blinking, she inclined her head the barest amount.

Not good enough, I thought.

"Say 'yes, Father Bell, I understand,'" I commanded.

It was either the demand that she call me by that name or the tone of voice that did it. The breath left her body in one ragged exhale, and she finally turned to face me, lifting her tear-streaked face to mine. For a moment, I thought maybe she wouldn't respond, or maybe she would tell me to leave, or maybe she'd resort to physically pushing me away.

She didn't do any of these things.

"Yes, Father Bell," she whispered instead. "I understand."

CHAPTER EIGHT

"My little lamb," I murmured, finally able to give in and touch her. I slid one hand around her neck, finding that stray tendril in back and curling it idly around one finger as I spoke. "The things I want to do to you…"

Her lush red lips parted. "If you do those things to me, you'll have to fight for them."

"Is that what you really want?" I asked, moving her silky hair between my fingertips. "Or is this your way of asking me to leave?"

"No," she said firmly. "I *want* you to fight me for it. I want to fuck you, and I want it to be rough. I just also wanted you to know that I'm so furious with you right now, and it makes me want to leave scratches all over your body."

I almost groaned at that. Every word she spoke made my cock throb painfully, and I was torn between jumping feet first into this hatefuck or dropping to my knees and begging her to put my dick out of its misery.

She cleared up that dilemma for me when she palmed my erection through my tuxedo pants, squeezing hard. "I want you to hurt when you come for me," she hissed.

"And I want to fucking tear you apart," I growled.

Her eyes flashed. "I'd like to see you try."

My hand was wrapped around her throat in an instant, pushing her back into the cold glass of the mirror. My other hand found her wrist and moved it above her head, but before I could properly pin it against the glass, she slapped me across the face—*hard*—the crack resounding through the small studio like a gunshot.

I staggered back—more surprised than hurt, and harder than ever—and she slipped from my grasp, ducking under my arm and bolting for the door. With the lacy skirt of her dress bunched in one hand and her gold heels shining in the moonlight, she looked like a princess out of a fairytale. This wasn't a fairytale, though, and even if it were, I certainly wasn't playing the role of prince tonight.

I caught up to her in a few long strides, grabbing her arm and spinning her around to face me. Her foot shot out, connecting with my shin, the bright flash of pain loosening my grip enough that she could try to pull away—*try* being the operative word. I reached for her waist and wrapped an arm around it, pulling her tight against me and pressing my erection into her stomach.

"You feel that?"

She squirmed against me, trying to wriggle free.

"That's for you, lamb," I told her, pinning her tighter against me, making her feel every inch of my hardness through our clothes. "It's all for you."

And then I kissed her, my mouth crashing against hers, and she moaned into my mouth, forgetting herself and opening her lips to me, letting my tongue flicker against hers. Everything about her was so soft right now—her mouth, her stomach against my steel-hard cock, the upper arm I still held tight in my grip.

So soft—

Four lines of pain, blazing and sharp, razored down my neck. I felt anger and lust and that uniquely visceral thrill that came from feeling as if I'd paid a penance, as if I'd endured a just punishment; I pulled back to see Poppy's eyes wide and feral in the light, her hand still raised.

Our gazes met. Blood welled hot out of one of the scratches, spilling over and down into my tuxedo shirt.

And then she tried to run again.

I managed to hold on to her enough that she only made it a step or two, and then the momentum took us both. We fell into a tangled pile of lace and legs and arms, and I struggled to regain a hold on her, but she was too fast, up on her hands and knees trying to crawl away, and I crawled after her, stretching out to wrap a strong hand around her ankle.

She shrieked in protest as I hauled her back to me,

climbing over her and trapping her body under mine. "Let's see what I've caught," I rasped in her ear, pinning both her wrists with one hand and then using my other hand to lift the skirt of her dress.

She kicked her legs and tried to twist away, but my position on top of her made escape impossible. Somewhere, in the back of my lust-addled mind, a messenger from my conscience revived. *Make sure she's still okay*, it demanded. *Check to see if she needs to stop.* After all, we'd had rough sex before, but never in anger. Never like this. This was uncharted territory.

My fingers paused at the edge of her silk panties. My hand shook with the effort of stopping; hell, my whole body shook with the effort of stopping. But I did it. One faint point in Good Guy Tyler's favor.

"Do you want me to stop, lamb?" I forced myself to ask. "I can stop."

Her mouth twisted into a victorious smile. "Why, are you afraid of losing?"

"I won't lose," I growled.

"Then shut the hell up and fuck me!" she panted. "I already told you I wanted it this way, what more do you need?"

Good Guy Tyler would probably need lots more things. But Good Guy Tyler wasn't here right now.

Father Bell was here instead. And church was in session.

Still holding her wrists to the floor, I started rubbing her clit over the silk of her panties, relishing the way her eyes fluttered shut when I found just the right pressure, just the right tempo, and she stopped tried to wriggle free, instead bucking her hips up to meet my hand. Even the outside of her panties were damp, which made me think of our heated moment in the loft, which made me think of Anton and the fact that I wasn't sure if he was still down here searching for Poppy or not. In a moment of renewed anger, I fisted one side of her underwear and tore them off her hips, shredding the delicate embroidered fabric and leaving her sweet cunt bare for me.

And then I spanked it.

She let out a little squeak, squirming away from me, and I spanked it again, just to hear her make that noise again. I got to my knees and straddled her waist, leaving her pussy wet and exposed behind me. With the hand not holding her wrists, I fumbled with my button and zipper, my dick springing free, dark and veined and so hard it ached.

"Open those red lips for me," I said.

"Make me."

I moved up her body and angled myself forward, the flared crown of my cock nudging against her lips, which were pressed firmly closed. "You want me to make you?" I threatened.

She raised an eyebrow in challenge.

Quick as a flash, I let go of her wrists and reached into the bodice of her dress, where I found an erect nipple and twisted. She cried out in mingled pain and pleasure, parting those lips, and I thrust my hips down at the same instant, shoving myself inside her mouth.

I let out a string of swear words the moment my dick was inside, pushing against her tongue. *Fuck* and *shit* and *Jesus, that feels so good*. I started moving in and out, and then I let go of her wrists to brace myself more heavily on the floor, my other hand tangling deep in her hair.

I shouldn't have let go.

She flipped onto one side, unsettling my balance and also removing her delicious mouth from my dick, and then she scrambled out from underneath me. I tried to hold onto her hair and then she was struggling with me, and I wasn't sure how she managed it, but there was another slap and then a shove so hard that I tumbled backwards, my head knocking against the wood floor. Adrenaline pounded through me, the urge to fight and to fuck, and then she was crawling up my body like a tigress, her face wild and sexy as hell with her slightly blurred lipstick and stray hair falling from her up-do.

She straddled me, pressing her bare pussy against my bare cock, and it was a twisted version of the first time we'd ever fooled around together, her rubbing herself against me while I grabbed her hips to move her harder and faster. But this time I wore a tux, not a priest's collar, and we were in Poppy's dance studio, not a church. And this time she swatted my hands away impatiently, moving her hand up to squeeze around my throat.

I stilled.

Everything was so wet where she was sitting on me, so fucking wet and warm, and then without warning, she was tucking her skirt in one elbow and then gripping my root and then moving up and *oh my fucking God oh my fucking God oh my fucking God.*

So tight. So wet. So fucking warm.

Her pussy enveloped me in one rough movement, and her hold on my throat tightened as she started fucking me harder than she'd ever fucked me before, taking me to the hilt and then bucking against me, the sweet pink berry of her clit rubbing against the muscle above my cock.

She moved violently, ferociously, punishing me for all of my sins—and fuck, if this was the punishment I deserved, then I would sin again and again and again. She wrapped her other hand around the lapel of my tux jacket, using the lapel and my throat for leverage, and she was like a woman possessed on top of me, riding me as hard as I'd wanted to ride her.

"Oh my God," I groaned, closing my eyes, barely able to breathe past her hand around my neck. I couldn't watch her any more, that needy clit or those red lips or that elegant hand holding my lapel in a death grip. It was all too much, I was far too worked up, and I could feel a biting, gnawing hurricane gathering at the base of my spine.

"Don't you dare come," she half-ordered, half-pleaded.

"Don't you fucking dare. Not yet."

I opened my eyes, and this time when I reached for her hips, she let me. I helped her move faster and harder, and it was only a few seconds more before her breathing grew ragged and her hips moved jerkily, a blush staining her chest and cheeks. And then she cried out, slumping forward onto me—her hand still fast around my throat—her pussy quivering in tight, squeezing flutters.

"Oh God," she was moaning, her face buried in my tuxedo jacket. "Holy fuck, holy fuck, holy fuck."

And that is when I noticed that I hadn't closed the door to the studio properly, leaving a small crack visible to the hallway. A shadow hovered in that hallway, a figure standing just to the side of the door. It only took one glance to confirm; Anton had finally found us. And he was watching.

Let's give him a show, a terrible version of myself thought. *Why don't you show him what it's like when you get to take what's yours to take?*

I flipped us over, Poppy's orgasm-weak hands sliding off of me as I started driving into her. I had one arm around her waist and the other holding my weight, but it wasn't enough, it wasn't deep enough or hard enough or fast enough. I wanted Anton to see how rough my lamb let me give it to her, I wanted him to be able to feel the force of my fucking her through the floor, through the walls. I wanted the whole studio to shake with it.

I pulled out and stood up, my dick like a thick, dark knife jutting out from my tux, and then I reached down and hauled her to her feet. She was unsteady and dazed, still panting and flushed from her climax, and she didn't protest as I walked around and tugged on the zipper to her dress.

Unzipped, the dress gaped in back, the straps threatening to slide off her shoulders, and I helped them along their way, stripping her completely naked, save for her strapless bra and heels. Poppy had once stripped for me in a club, and had stripped for me privately many times since, but those times, she'd been in complete control of her body and her sex. Those times, she'd held all the power, all the control.

Not this time.

This time, there was an undercurrent of darkness, of all the most misogynistic and prideful impulses a man can have for a woman. I wanted her to *feel* naked, vulnerable and humiliated, and I wanted Anton to witness it. I wanted him to see every inch of her sweet, perfect body and know that it all belonged to me, to use or degrade however I wanted. It was beyond sinful, it was borderline evil, and even the dim recognition of how terrible it was only served to inflame me more.

"Take off your bra," I demanded hoarsely, still behind her and looking down at her chest from over her shoulder.

Shaking, she obeyed me, reaching behind her back and then letting the small black bra fall loose. I let out a short, heavy breath at the sight of her breasts—sweet and full and ripe and pink at the tips. I stepped closer, grinding my erection against her ass while my hands found her tits, palming them with rough, hard movements. Around us, the mirrors reflected every angle of our bodies ad infinitum, a never-ending tunnel of my tuxedo and her ivory skin and my hands so cruelly pulling and squeezing.

"Look," I whispered in her ear, hoping Anton was looking too. "Look in the mirrors. Can you see yourself?"

She nodded against me, her eyes on the mirror directly across from us, where she watched one of my hands drift down to her stomach and then lower and lower, until my middle finger began stroking her clit. She squirmed.

"I want you to watch me fuck you. I want you to see what I see when I fuck you, what other people would see if they were watching us." *Since we are being watched*, I almost added but didn't. This was between me and Anton, this struggle for possession. Poppy didn't need to know.

I pointed to the closest wall, where a two-tiered barre was installed against the floor-to-ceiling mirror. She knew without me elaborating what I wanted, and she walked over to the barre, letting her hands settle onto the wood as she took a deep breath.

She watched me approach in the mirror, and when I got close enough, I gave her ass a firm smack. "Foot up on the barre, lamb. I want to see that cunt."

She lifted her foot, the gold heel tumbling off and falling

to the floor, and then she extended her leg, resting her ankle on the barre. So now she stood on one heel, both hands braced on the barre, and with one leg stretched out to the side. All completely naked.

I rubbed the head of my cock at her wet entrance, digging my fingers into her hips as I angled my body and slowly pushed into her pussy. "Watch it, lamb. Watch." I reached up and found her face, forcing her to look at the mirror to her side, where the reflection perfectly framed my dick thrusting up into her.

She shuddered at the sight. "Tyler," she said breathlessly. "I'm going to—oh God."

"Not yet," I said, leaning back a little so I could enjoy my own view better. "Isn't that what you said to me earlier? Well, I'm saying it to you now. Not yet. Not until I'm pumping you full of my cum."

"Jesus," she mumbled, her head falling forward. "I don't think I can wait."

I was still watching my glistening dick pull out of and then push into that tight, pink pussy, that pussy that was so deliciously open in this position. With her leg up on the barre, I could hit her deep inside, and with the mirror in front of her, I could see every fleeting smile, every silent gasp, and it made me almost crazed to see how good she was feeling when I was being so very, very bad to her.

"You like it when I use you like this?" I asked her. "When I strip you and humiliate you?"

"Yes," was all she could manage. Her tits bounced and the muscles in her thighs were bunched with the strain of this position, and that jagged heat was at the base of my spine, and then deep in my pelvis, and then exploding inside me and through me, with all the heat and shearing force of a hydrogen bomb.

I should find her clit and rub it hard, I should make sure she comes again, but holy fuck, it felt so good and I needed this so bad, needed to fill her up with me, needed to release, needed to fuck her blind. And so I pounded into her as my climax shredded through my body, pounded her so hard that she fell forward, her face pressed into the glass of the mirror, and then she was screaming my name, screaming God's name, as her channel contracted around me. Her support leg gave out and so in the end it was only my hands gripping into her hips that kept her upright as I drained my balls into her, not easing up until I knew every last drop was inside of her, until every pulse and throb of my dick had finally, finally stilled.

I stayed there just a second more, not moving, just feeling the heat of my climax inside of her, just staring at her flushed, sated face—which was still pressed against the mirror—and simply savoring every toned, taut line of her body. It was with the utmost reluctance that I pulled out, severing our connection and dispelling whatever magic and fury had taken hold of us in here.

I hoped Anton had seen every second of it, but when I

glanced at the door, he was gone. I gently set Poppy back onto her feet, helping her find the lost heel, and then when we both straightened and our eyes met, it crashed into me, sharp and explosive.

The guilt.

The shame.

The knowledge of what I had just done—from being late to the gala, to my gnawing jealousy, to my using my lamb like a whore, just to prove a point to another man. And to prove something to her and also to myself, and fuck.

I'd fucked up.

I wasn't looking in the mirror right now, but if I was, I wouldn't recognize the man standing there.

He wasn't a priest.

He wasn't a good man, and he certainly wasn't a good husband. And when I looked into Poppy's newly tearful hazel eyes, I knew that nothing was okay.

CHAPTER NINE

I was immediately consumed by the need to confess. To fall to my knees and spill every terrible, selfish urge and thought, to purge it all in front of her and for her, because I could see this wound in her eyes, a wound that I'd just worsened, and I had to fix it. I had to atone.

"Poppy—"

She shook her head. "Give me a moment, Tyler."

I fell silent.

She took a deep breath. She was still completely naked, but it no longer mattered, because a distance was slowly settling in her eyes, along with a cold, elegant posture and a composed press of her lips—she wore an invisible armor that did far more to separate us than clothes ever could.

I tried again, desperate to keep this chasm from opening wider. "I'm so sorry, lamb. I thought you wanted it—"

"Give me a fucking minute!" Her voice started out quiet

and collected, but then quickly escalated into a quavering yell, which reverberated against the studio floors and walls and also inside of my chest. She glanced away, breathing out and breathing in again. Then she turned back to me. "I did want it," she said, calmer now. "And I wanted it like that. Rough and hard. Please trust me when I tell you what I want, and please trust me to tell you to stop if I need it. I'm frankly tired of having to give you explicit permission every single time we do something kinkier than kiss. I like being fucked that way, and tonight was no exception."

"But you don't know what I was thinking when I was fucking you—"

She let out a long breath, her jaw setting. "I knew exactly what you were thinking. I saw Anton too."

Oh shit.

"Poppy…" She didn't interrupt me, but I still stopped, because what could I say?

"The thing is, I didn't mind it. I thought it was kind of sexy, actually. You fucking me while he watched. And you want to know why?"

Please don't say it's because you find him attractive. Please don't say it's because you want him.

"He was watching because he finds *you* impossibly sexy, and so I imagine it made his night. It's hot to me because I love it when anybody—no matter who they are—notices how sexy my Father Bell is."

My mouth was dry and my mind whirled with this new

information. "I don't understand," I said, blinking a little. "Anton…?"

"Is bisexual," Poppy confirmed. "And has had a little crush on you since he met you a couple years ago."

"I just…I didn't know…" I felt like such an idiot, wasting so much time being jealous and angry. Over nothing.

Poppy bent down to get her bra and dress off the floor, and her movements were jerky and stilted, and I realized that Anton was not the issue here, at least not for her.

"What is it?" I asked, hoping against hope that she would tell me and not storm out.

She straightened up, fastening her bra and not looking at me. "This usually works," she said, and her voice sounded choked. "We fight and we screw and then everything is fine. I thought it would work tonight—I thought this is what I needed to feel better. To have you use me, to have you make me come. But it's not better right now."

"Because of the gala?"

"Because of everything. When we met, you were a priest and so you were putting everyone first, never thinking about yourself or what you needed. And I was so proud to be the woman who could coax selfishness out of you, who could coax you to take what you wanted."

I knew immediately what she was saying. "I never meant to put myself first tonight, Poppy. It was Professor Morales and her baby, and please, lamb—"

She was shaking her head, her hands trembling as she put her dress back on, barely able to manage the zipper but stepping away when I tried to help. "It's not just tonight, Tyler. It's been this entire year, and I *can't* anymore. I asked you for one thing—for one time. I asked you for tonight, because even though you've been a ghost all this year, I thought maybe if you came tonight and saw everything I've worked so hard for, that it would make up for it all. But now I think it wouldn't have, no matter what you did or didn't do."

I reached for her and I didn't let her wriggle away this time, keeping her shoulders tight in my hands and searching her face. "Tell me how to fix this," I pleaded. "I know I've fucked up and I keep fucking up, but things can get better. They *will* get better—my dissertation defense is this week and then all this craziness will be over."

"You really think it will make a difference?" she snapped. "You think you'll be able to magically throw yourself back into being a husband?"

I was almost speechless. "Of course, Poppy. This is just a season!"

"Don't give me that 'season' bullshit. You know what I think? I think that you will always be chasing after the next thing, the next vocation, the next escape. First a priest...then a scholar...don't you see that you're doing everything you can to hide from being just Tyler Bell, a person and not a title?"

"That's not fair," I protested, sputtering. "I don't use jobs to *hide* from anything!"

"I need you to be a part of my life, and I'm not sure that you're capable of that anymore," she continued, not listening to me. "I'm beginning to think that you just want to be alone."

"Jesus Christ, Poppy. No. A thousand times no, that is not what I want! I want you!"

"Then why won't you stand by my side when I need you?" Tears streamed down her face. "Why do I have to eat alone, go to sleep alone, put up Christmas trees alone? This was supposed to be the beginning of our new chapter, this was supposed to be our next big moment—"

I was confused. "What? This gala?"

"Fuck the gala!" she cried. "Of course you have no idea what I'm talking about because you haven't been anywhere around me when I've needed you. It's like you don't love me—"

"Goddammit, Poppy, I left my church for you!"

The words, angry and bitter, resounded in the enclosed room, echoing and drowning out every other noise. I hadn't meant to say it, but it had burst out of me all the same, and once I said it, I knew that the damage had been done. To her and to me, because the party line—the thing we told curious acquaintances and friends—had always been that I'd left the church for me and for no other reason.

And it was more than the party line, it was the truth.

Except now I wondered if maybe it wasn't the whole truth, and if this was just the first time I'd admitted it to myself.

And in Poppy's eyes, I could tell that I had just confirmed every unspoken fear she'd ever had about us.

She took a step backward into the dark. "I need some time to think," she said emotionlessly. "Please don't be home when I go back there tonight."

No, I wanted to say. *I want to fix this.* I couldn't imagine spending the night—all night—apart from her right now. I couldn't imagine letting this wound fester and become infected with resentment and unexplained truths.

God helped me in that moment, the slightest note of clarity in the midst of my pain and confusion. A tiny drop of peace, of *you can do this, if only for her sake.*

"How long do you want me to stay away?" I asked and then I realized I was crying too.

Poppy's tears mirrored my own, but her voice was still flat and without affect when she said, "I don't know. Maybe a week. Maybe more."

My chest cracked open and my heart fell out.

"A week?" I whispered disbelievingly.

"I'll call or text when I'm ready to talk." And without anything more, without an *I love you* or even a *goodbye*, she walked out.

I went home and packed a bag. Realistically I knew that

she would stay longer at the gala, and that even if she didn't, she wouldn't come inside while my truck was in the driveway, but I still hoped that she'd walk in while I was here. That she'd run in, having changed her mind, and then she'd let me apologize. She'd let me fall to my knees and confess, and then after I confessed, she would let me atone. I'd whip myself for her. I'd walk across broken glass and hot coals for her, climb up on a cross for her...although my intentions were still less than Christlike.

Anger shadowed my guilt, anger and blame, and I knew that my desire to atone came not just from guilt, but from a desire to hurt her by hurting myself.

Not Christlike at all.

In the end, it didn't matter. Poppy never came home. I packed my bag, looked around the townhouse, and then left for the closest hotel, which was a cheap, anonymous place with a squeaky bed and a framed picture of a spoon.

I knew she said she'd call me when she was ready, so out of respect for her boundaries, I didn't call.

But I wrote.

I wrote by hand, which was something I'd never done in my adult life, writing her my first letter on some Post-It notes I'd found in my laptop bag. I delivered it the next day on my way to Mass, sliding the paper-clipped Post-Its through the mail slot in the door. Her little Fiat was nowhere in sight and I hoped that meant she'd be at Mass, that I could at least fill some of this void with a glimpse of her face.

She wasn't there. Poppy never missed Mass unless she was traveling or sick, but that day, she was absent, and I knew it was because of me. Because she was avoiding me.

I wrote her another letter during the service, this time on the back of the church newsletter. I delivered that and I went to the library to work the day away and lose my mind in ancient theology. (It didn't work. I couldn't stop thinking about Poppy and our fight.)

I fell into the kind of miserable routine that stretches hours into years. At night, I lay between thin, foreign sheets and stared at the ceiling, waiting for sleep to come. During the day, I sunk myself into the final pages of my dissertation, trying to push down the oppressive torment of missing my wife.

We'd never fought like this, *never*, not in three years of marriage, and I had no idea how to fix things. I had no idea how to prove to her that I would be better, that I would be worthy, because I was still reeling from it all. Poppy had seemed so understanding, so patiently calm, all this year, but had it been a front all along? Had she been gathering this pain and anger under the surface for the last twelve months? Or had something changed just in the last week to ignite her pain?

And how could I possibly ever find out if she wouldn't speak to me?

On Tuesday, I went to the soup kitchen and worked silently, a zombie. And I was a zombie on the phone with

Millie on the way back home, which was fine, because she was quiet too. She didn't even complain about the food at Pinewoods Village.

"How is Poppy?" she finally asked after an exceptionally long pause.

There was no point in lying. "We're…we're having some difficulties."

"Are those difficulties your fault or hers?"

Snow flurried around me as I parked the truck in the faculty lot and trudged to my office. "Mostly mine."

Millie didn't say anything for a moment, but she did let out a few of those strange coughs that made me cringe to listen to.

"Millie, have you told a nurse that you haven't been feeling well?"

"They know," she said dismissively. "It's just a cold. Everyone gets them this time of year. Besides, I'm so sick of having them fuss over me. I miss being in my own home."

"I know you do."

More silence. A cough. "Sometimes I think it's not worth it to be here."

Her words sank through the murk of my depression and began pinging soft alarms in my mind. I stopped at the door to the building, my hand on the handle, snow drifting around me. "Millie, what do you mean by that?"

"Oh nothing. Just an old lady's rambles, that's all. I'll keep you and Poppy in my prayers this week."

"Okay, Millie. And I'll be praying for your cough."

After we exchanged goodbyes, I stepped inside the building and typed out a couple quick texts to Mom and Jordan, asking if they could check on Millie this week. Mom always did, but I wanted Jordan there too. He could tell right away if someone was soul-sick, and that's what I worried about with Millie. More than a cough, soul-sickness could kill someone like her, someone who needed a sense of purpose and independence to live.

Both Jordan and Mom responded with assurances that they would check on my old friend, and so I headed to my office to meet with a couple students and then I spent the rest of my day in the library, writing Poppy letters that she would probably never read and plodding through the last several thousand words of my conclusion.

And so the week went on, each day worse than the last, each day that Poppy didn't call or text like a fresh version of hell, and I became a shadow of myself. Not eating, barely sleeping, my focus so intent on Poppy and what she was doing at each moment that I couldn't attend to anything else.

It was a miracle that I made it to my dissertation.

It was an even bigger miracle that I could force myself to speak words, sentences, coherent thoughts. I was glad Professor Morales was on maternity leave, because I didn't want her to see me like this. Fucked up and clumsy, and lackluster in my defense, even as the board members raved about my conclusion and how practical and visionary it was. Morales would have been proud of that part, at least.

And then the biggest miracle of all: I made it through. As Jesus said, *it is finished*, and so I walked out of that building with my doctorate in theology, four years of my life finally sealed shut and packed away. I was supposed to be happy now, I knew. I was supposed to be giddy with my accomplishment and the chance for a new phase in my life.

But I was also supposed to be celebrating with my wife right now. I was supposed to be kissing her, holding her, whispering wild promises in her ear.

Instead, I ate a greasy dinner alone in a mostly-empty restaurant, watching Christmas shoppers pass by the window, listening to holiday songs so familiar and overplayed that they'd become meaningless background noise peculiar to this one time of year—no more notable than cicadas chirruping in the summer heat or raindrops pattering against the window in the springtime. Just the noise that goes along with cold wet weather and the smell of gingerbread.

I went back to my hotel, turned on the shower and stripped down slowly, climbing in and sitting on the floor of the tub. I didn't cry, though. I just sat, empty and worthless, feeling the water sluicing across my skin like so much rain, and trying not to remember all the showers that Poppy and I had shared. All the wet kisses. All the skin and steam and breathy moans echoing off the tile.

Did I make a mistake leaving the clergy?

The thought surfaced out of nowhere, fractured and shifting like a reflection on the sea. But once it appeared, it couldn't be unthought, no matter how fleeting or ephemeral it had been.

When I'd left, I'd felt so certain, so confident that I was following God's plan for my life. That I was setting my feet to the path that would lead to self-actualizaton and modern-day sainthood and a full, rich life. I was so certain that it didn't matter what happened between me and Poppy, it didn't matter where the road took me, it only mattered that I step outside the safe bubble I'd made for myself and start taking real risks again.

There was no whisper of that confidence now, no lingering scent of that certainty. Because if all of my pain and effort meant that I was a PhD sitting alone in a shower, then what had all of it been for? What had the world gained by me leaving the clergy?

Poppy was right—I liked to hide behind vocations, behind callings—and *scholar* was so much worse than *priest* because at least priests helped people. At least they brought people closer to the Lord. Everything I'd gained as a student, I'd gained for myself. It hadn't even netted anything positive for my marriage.

And if Poppy left me, actually left me and filed for divorce, I would break. Not just my heart, and not just my mind, but my soul and my body—it would splinter into brittle dead shards and I would be finished.

Lord, where are you? I asked the ceiling numbly. *Why do I feel so alone?*

And that was when the phone rang.

CHAPTER TEN

I scrambled out of the tub, grabbing a towel and running into the hotel room. My phone was lit up and buzzing its way across the end table.

Please let this be the answer to my prayer.

Please let this be Poppy.

Please, Lord. Please please please.

But the moment I saw the 816 area code, I knew it wasn't Poppy. My heart—which had been pounding like mad, full of hope and energy and nervousness—flopped down to somewhere in my stomach.

Even though it was an unfamiliar number, I still made myself answer.

"Hello?"

A pause. "Is this Tyler Bell?"

I scrubbed my face with the towel while I answered. "Yes. How can I help?"

"I'm Sarah Russell, Mildred Gustaferson's daughter."

I let the towel fall away from my face. "Millie? Is everything okay?"

Sarah didn't answer right away, but when she did, she was obviously fighting back tears. "I'm sorry to be the one to tell you this. My mother died this morning."

I flew to Kansas City alone.

I'd broken my self-enforced phone fast and called Poppy. She hadn't answered. I'd left a voicemail and sent a text, and then I'd driven to our house before I went to the airport, hoping to catch her there, knowing that she would want to know about Millie.

She hadn't been home.

And so I was alone on the plane, my eyes pressed tightly shut, as if I could keep the tears from falling that way. But they still managed to leak out, slowly and ceaselessly, hot tracks of grief and isolation against my cheeks. I felt so hollow and yet so full, so blank and yet so scrawled upon by events outside my control. My good friend dying, my wife's absence, this ridiculous distance between me and all the people I cared about. Nothing felt real, nothing felt intimate or close or true—it all seemed like a terrible movie of my life that I was being forced to watch from hundreds of feet away.

When I stared out the airplane window, my reflection superimposed against the velvet night outside, I barely recognized the unshaven man there. Who was he? Where was he going? And why was he going there alone?

The questions were too painful. I shut the shade for the window and leaned back, closing my eyes again, hoping to keep back a fresh wave of tears.

The priest in me wanted to meditate right now. He wanted to pray. He wanted to think of the right things to say to Millie's children when he went to the funeral, and he wanted to have the right verses ready in his mind in case they were needed.

But the other me—the guy who was Just Tyler—wanted to do nothing at all, except maybe flag the stewardess for a drink. He wanted to think about nothing, feel nothing, say nothing, and do you know what?

That's exactly what he did.

"Your tie is crooked."

I turned back to my brother's bedroom mirror. "It is not!"

Sean huffed impatiently. "The knot is crooked. Hang on."

I let him fiddle with my tie some more, my thoughts elsewhere. Well, on one thing in particular. Poppy still hadn't called me back. She wasn't here and she hadn't called or texted and I had no idea still if she even knew about Millie. And since it was the day of the funeral, I'd given up on the faint but unflagging hope that she'd fly out here to be with me.

"There," Sean said, stepping back and gazing at the Windsor knot he'd just made with a critical eye. "Better."

Sean himself looked every inch the impeccable mourner, his tailored black suit and his Charvet tie screaming money and power. Since I'd left the clergy four years ago, he'd risen to the top of his investment firm, which had in turn become one of the biggest Midwestern firms in America, handling massive agricultural and livestock accounts, along with the private accounts of several Midwestern professional athletes. We were probably as different as two brothers could be—me, the priest-turned-scholar, and him, the millionaire playboy who only went to Mass when someone died—but we looked like a matching set in our black suits. His hair was a dark blond to my brown and his eyes were a blue to my green, but we shared the same high cheekbones and square jaw, the same mouth that maybe smiled a little too widely, the same dimples that dug into our cheeks when that wide smile did appear.

And for all that he was a shallow, self-obsessed asshole, he had genuinely cared about Millie. She'd sent him cookies every month since I'd moved to her parish, and he'd adopted her as a sort-of grandma slash financial advisor, bringing his iPad full of business proposals for her to run through whenever he'd visited her. Aiden, our younger brother, had cared about her too, but he was on a business trip in Brussels and couldn't make it back for her funeral.

"So," Sean said as we walked into the elevator down to where his Audi waited. "Where's your fucking wife, TinkerBell?"

It was like simultaneous shots of rubbing alcohol and laughing gas. For a moment, irritation and raw hurt blinded me…and then I couldn't help but laugh. Mom and Dad, and even my teenaged brother Ryan, sensed it was a delicate subject for me and so had danced around Poppy's absence like one would dance around a live grenade. But Sean—Sean gave no fucks about anybody else's feelings, and hadn't since our sister had hung herself in our parents' garage all those years ago. It was the best and worst thing about him, and right now, it was exactly what I needed.

"I think she is really angry with me," I said. The elevator got to the parking garage level and we walked towards Sean's car. "I think…I think we might not be together anymore."

Sean looked at me. It wasn't a look of pity or concern, necessarily, but a look of understanding. A look of *even if we don't talk, even if we don't share our adult lives together, I'm still here for you.* I guess that was the thing about brothers. We shared something that couldn't be artificially minted or molted away, a bond that would stick for as long as we were both alive.

"You know," Sean said slowly, looking at me over the hood of the car, "if you need anything or—like—to talk, I'm here."

Gratitude and affection for my asshole brother flooded me. I knew those words didn't come naturally or easily to him. "Thanks, Sean. I'll let you know if I need anything."

He nodded and then got in the Audi. The matter was settled, and it was time to hit the road. Millie had wanted her last rites at St. Margaret's, the parish she'd given so much of her life to, and that meant a drive to Weston from Kansas City, which was about an hour long.

When we got to St. Margaret's, we parked the car and Sean went inside to find Mom. I made the excuse that I wanted to walk around and see the new rectory, but really I just needed a moment alone. I poked and prodded at the empty hole in my chest, the place where my wife had lived and then slid out of, like a snake sliding out of its old skin. And I also prodded the thick cloud of grief hovering in my mind, the cloud made of homemade casseroles and long phone calls and hours of working the soup kitchen together.

I've heard people say that losing someone as old as Millie is easier. That all the time they lived and the time you've shared makes the loss not such a burden, not so weighted with what ifs. But I didn't feel like that today. Five hundred years wouldn't be enough to contain all the potential of a woman like Millie Gustaferson, much less ninety-two. And without her, I was without one of my strongest links to the man I used to be.

The worst thing was that I knew something was off when I talked to her last Tuesday. I should have done more—called the Pinewoods Village director or found the number for one of her children. Mom and Jordan had both visited, and while Jordan told me that she'd been listless and obviously depressed, neither felt like she was in any real danger.

Pneumonia was the official cause of death. But unofficially, her kids told me, there was another element. She'd hidden how severe the illness was from her nurses and her visitors, and by the time Thursday morning dawned, she was gasping and blue and it was too late for the antibiotics to have any real effect.

Sometimes I think it's not worth it to be here, she'd said. Had she indirectly tried to kill herself by hiding how sick she was?

And how depressed was I that I completely understood how she felt?

I rubbed my cheeks with my hands and took a deep breath. I was too familiar with death from my days as a priest to succumb to the need for explanations and narratives about the deceased's last days. Death has no narrative.

It just is.

With that cheerful thought, I finally got out of the car and walked into the church that I'd walked into a thousand times before. Everywhere there were signs of change. The new priest's picture in the foyer next to a list of office hours. Christmas lights and trees a week earlier than I would have put them up. The smell of bread wafting from the kitchen downstairs, when I'd always preferred the evocative smell of incense, and kept some burning almost at all times.

And then there was the building itself. When I'd worked here, the walls had been paneled with fake wood and the carpet had been a dull red—holdovers from a gruesome mid-century renovation. But now the building was exactly what I'd always hoped it would become—modern and light and clean. The walls had been stripped to their original 19th Century brick and stone and the carpet had vanished, replaced by wide planks of blond wood. Pendant lamps of brushed aluminum hung from the ceiling, accented by the old stained glass that had been restored to its original glory. And in the far corner, a glass and concrete baptismal font sat shimmering in the dim December light, water spilling over the inside edges like an infinity pool, filling the church with the gentle music of running water.

St. Margaret's finally had a building to match her beautiful, passionate congregation. A building a world apart from the scandal that had rocked the town the year before I came, apart from the old, closed-in mindset of the 20th Century church. Light and modernity and openness—Pope Francis's church. Father Bell's church.

Except it wasn't Father Bell's. It was Father McCoy's now.

But that was the beauty of the church, really. The priests may change, the congregants may pass away, but the church was still there. The church endured, a steadfast house of solace and refuge for all that come seeking.

The church kept its doors open. Even when its priests left. *Knock and the door shall be opened to you*, Jesus had promised. Although it felt like I'd been knocking all week and the door to Poppy's heart had remained as tightly shut and intransigent as ever.

I bit down my urge to criticize Father McCoy during the service. Of course, I would always feel like I could do better, like St. Margaret's was mine and mine alone, and so I didn't need to inwardly groan every time he stumbled over a word or lost pitch while chanting the call and response songs. It was fine. Even if it was the funeral of one of the smartest and best women in the world, it was still fine that he was mediocre.

Fine, fine, fine.

By the time the Mass had almost finished and it was time for me to deliver my eulogy, I'd torn my funeral program into tiny, frustrated pieces. I craved Poppy, Millie was dead, and the priest was terrible. What else could a man endure? When I stood to go to the front, Mom cleared her throat quietly and held out her cupped hands for me to dump my piles of shredded program into.

Good old Mom.

The walk to the front felt strange. I'd come down this center aisle so many times, robed and collared and processing behind a cross, and now I was in a civilian's suit, walking on unfamiliar floors while unfamiliar lights dangled above me.

It should have been me performing her Mass, a petulant part of me thought. What good were you to Millie if you couldn't even perform her last Mass? Was it worth it? Leaving the church?

Was it?

Well, was it?

I didn't have an answer to that any more. Plus one degree, minus one wife. Net profit: zero.

I climbed up to the lectern and got behind it, looking out over the crowd as I pulled up my notes on my phone. "So...this feels familiar."

Several people in the pews laughed despite their tears. Most of the people here had been my flock, and while I knew there was no ill will over my leaving or the way I had left, I still wished I could know what they were thinking as they looked up at me now, standing behind my old lectern.

"We all knew Millie well," I started, gazing out at the mourners. "And I think no one was surprised to walk in and find a bright purple casket with the Kansas State Wildcat painted on the side. Millie, I know you can hear me from heaven right now, and *rock chalk, Jayhawk.*"

More laughter. I looked down at my notes, notes I'd written in Sean's penthouse while gazing out at the gray winter sky. Notes that I'd written thinking about my last night with Poppy, when I'd told her I knew her better than any other person alive.

"Today is a day where we mourn and miss the Millie we

all knew. But I want to take a minute and think about all the things we didn't know. The things we'll never know now. Whether she liked to keep her hand on the remote while she watched television. Whether she waited for her coffee to brew in the kitchen or whether she did other things while it brewed instead. Whether she preferred her crossword in the morning or at night. We might remember her favorite meal, her favorite hymn…which candidate she sent nasty letters to during the last election."

Laughter again, because yeah, we all knew that one for sure.

"But a person is so much more than those big things. A person is a collection of small things, of tiny invisible moments, of thoughts too inconsequential to share, of feelings that are too petty not to hide. Of glorious epiphanies too perfect to taint by speaking them out loud. And the real tragedy is not just that we won't ever get to know these things about Millie. It's that we so rarely take the time to know them about each other."

My throat tightened as I thought about Poppy.

"When you go home tonight, look at the people around you. And search for those secrets. Millie would want you to hold on to them, those fleeting insubstantial moments. That was one of her gifts: seeing people how they really are."

I paused, because I was at the end of my notes, but looking out at the crowd—all crying again—I didn't want to leave them like this. I wanted to leave this lectern with levity and with laughter. For Millie. So I leaned down and murmured, "And her other gift was casseroles," which earned the loudest laughter of all, but I didn't even care at that point because when I lifted my eyes to the back of the sanctuary, I saw a slender woman clad all in black with dark hair and red lips, and it was like lightening striking me where I stood.

Poppy had come after all.

CHAPTER
ELEVEN

By the time I left the lectern, Poppy was gone. Behind me, I could hear Father McCoy beginning the final prayers and farewells that would wrap up the service, and it would be disrespectful and rude to simply walk out of the sanctuary at this point, but I didn't care. I had to find her, and I also knew that Millie would have wanted me to do the same thing.

The narthex was empty except for a couple of children chasing each other around the fonts of holy water. Their shouts and squeaks were incongruous with the heavy atmosphere just inside the sanctuary, but also perfect. Millie loved children; she would have wanted them happy and playing at her funeral, and so despite the fact that I was hunting for my wife with my heart jackhammering at a million miles per hour, I smiled at them. Smiled and wished that I could count on a future where I would have loud children running around a church, happy and playing, and ours.

I pushed the outside doors open, the bitter wind bringing with it tiny pellets of ice and sleet. Even though it was only four in the afternoon, the sun was setting, and already the Christmas lights along Weston's main strip of antique shops and wineries were lit up. The glow gave the scene a homey, cozy feeling despite the desolate sky and the brownish river bluffs in the distance.

"Tyler," came a quiet, shivering voice.

Poppy stood at the edge of the steps outside the door. Rosy spots had blossomed high on her cheeks and her breath came in large white clouds. She wore a black-netted veil, which hung down to her chin, pinned with small ruby-encrusted combs into the graceful sweep of her hair. With her tailored coat and heels, she looked like a femme fatale from some 1930s noir drama, and I wanted to lift that veil and kiss that deadly red mouth. I was too tired for anger or defensiveness any longer.

A kiss would be enough.

But I kept my physical urges under control. "I'm so glad you came. It would have meant a lot to Millie."

She nodded, her eyes on the twinkling lights down the street. "And it meant a lot to me to be here. I cared about her too, you know."

A few days ago, a whole host of angry responses would have been hot and waiting on my tongue, but not today.

Instead I tore my eyes away from her face and pinned them on the salt-strewn steps. *We need to talk about our future,* I wanted to say. Or maybe the less threatening *we need to talk about us.* Or maybe simply *can I buy you a cup of coffee?*

She beat me to it. "I flew in this morning. I'd like to get a hotel room together, if that's okay with you?"

A fragile needle of hope pierced through my grief-haze. "Yes," I said softly. "Yes, that's okay with me."

We stayed for the funeral reception in the church basement, sharing stories of Millie and her life, and even Poppy spoke up a few times, although it was usually to add a small detail to what someone else was saying. After we ate our fill of potato-chip casseroles and pasta salads, we climbed into Sean's Audi. He gave me a look after Poppy climbed in, a *what the fuck is going on* look, but I ignored him. Mostly because I didn't trust that he wouldn't be an asshole to Poppy in the car, but also because I didn't know what was going on myself.

We swung by Sean's place to get my bag, and then he dropped us off at an expensive hotel downtown. When I made a noise of protest, he interrupted. "I'm taking care of it," he said firmly.

"Sean, man, I can't let you do that."

He shrugged. "I would like to see you stop me, given that I'm driving."

I flipped him off.

He punched my shoulder as I got out of the car and went to grab our things. After I helped Poppy out of the car, we walked inside the lobby and rented a room.

She was silent the whole time, somber and inexpressive in her netted veil and black clothes, and when we made it up to our room, she took off her coat and kicked off her heels without saying a word.

What was I supposed to do now? Was I supposed to ignore her? Ask her what's wrong? Tackle her to the bed and fuck her until we were both too tired to move anymore?

I didn't want to do any of those things, however, even the fucking. I put our bags on the floor and walked over to her, noticing the way she both tensed and canted toward me at the same time. She had to be as conflicted as I was, as torn apart by warring feelings, and everything about her screamed loneliness and unhappiness.

"Say 'red' if it gets to be too much," I murmured.

"Okay," she whispered. The first words she'd spoken to me since the funeral.

I used one finger to slowly lift her veil past her lips, past her nose, past her eyes. And then I leaned in and brushed my lips against hers.

Electricity, hot and tingling, spread from my mouth to the rest of my body, and she parted her lips, a small helpless noise escaping her as she leaned into my chest. I kept holding her veil up with one hand and then I slid the other behind her back, pulling her closer. But I didn't open my own lips, I didn't probe her tongue with mine. I simply kept our lips pressed together, sharing skin and sharing breath, until I pulled away and lowered her veil.

Her breathing was ragged, and I knew her body craved more, but I wasn't willing to exploit that. It was her heart and mind I was after, and I was too worn out and depressed to settle for anything less.

I reached up to her hair and slid out the delicate combs that held up her veil. And then I gently tugged her black blazer from her shoulders, drawing a shuddering inhale from her when my palms brushed against her stiffening nipples. I ignored the sigh (and the nipples) and focused on untucking her silk blouse, moving to the back to work on the small pearl buttons at the neck, and then I helped her out of it, followed by her skirt. Her stockings and garter belt were next, and goose bumps followed my fingers wherever they went, but I never touched her where I didn't need to. My hands and eyes stayed focused on the clothing, even when I unhooked her bra and tugged her silk thong down to her feet.

She stood completely naked before me, jaw set with the effort of controlling her breathing, and I left her for a moment, to get her bag. Setting it on the table next to me, I dug through it until I found what I was looking for: her makeup kit. I used the wipes and gently, methodically cleaned her face. I wiped off the kohl eyeliner and mascara, the bronzer she used because she was self-conscious about being so pale, the crimson lipstick. When I was done, I ran a thumb over those naked lips, sweet and full and parted ever so slightly by her teeth.

She blinked up at me, her face fresh and clean. "I thought when you said *red* that meant…"

I shook my head. "Not tonight."

"Tyler."

I pulled her silk robe out of her bag and slid it onto her, belting the sash securely. Once that was finished, I met her eyes and decided to be honest. She had to know why I couldn't fuck her safely tonight. "If I let myself go right now, it won't be pretty. I'll use that sash to gag you and two of my belts to fasten your ankles to those table legs over there. Then I'll lean you over that table and fuck you so hard you cry."

She swallowed, her pupils wide.

I ducked my head so she was forced to meet my eyes. "Is that what you want right now? Is that what you want tonight to be? All of my hurt and my grief directed at you?"

She grabbed my hand and dragged it under her robe. "I'm so wet for you," she pleaded. "Please."

My dick jolted but I stayed the course. I picked her up and carried her to bed, tucking her under the covers while I toed off my shoes and shrugged off my coat and tie. I left the dress shirt and slacks on, however, wanting more barriers between Poppy and me. I didn't trust myself not to exploit her arousal otherwise, even though I knew that fucking her would only complicate things more.

I crawled into bed next to her. "Remember to say red," I reminded her. And then I pulled her into me, so that our bodies lay flush together, my body curled around hers.

"This is hardly *red*-worthy," she said after a moment.

"You spent the last week avoiding me, lamb. I think letting me take care of you and then spending the night in my arms is a lot more difficult than being fucked."

And I was right. Because at some point in the night, a few hours after we'd fallen asleep, I woke up to the sound of her soft crying. She'd turned, so that her face was pressed against my shirt, and I cradled her there, running my hands through her hair and across her back while her tears spilled on my chest. I didn't ask her what was wrong, I didn't ask her *anything*, I just held her and stroked her until her crying grew quieter and quieter and she eventually drifted back into sleep.

I didn't go back to sleep, though. I stayed wide awake, wishing I knew what she'd been thinking about, what had made her cry, what had caused her sudden shift in temperament last week.

Maybe I'd never know. Maybe this was how I lived now, on the outskirts of her emotions, too close to leave but too far away to help.

I held her tighter at that thought. No. I wouldn't be on the periphery. I had to know whether she wanted me back inside…or if she wanted me gone altogether.

We had lunch with my parents, and then we were flying back home. She was just as quiet as she'd been yesterday, although she sought out my touch more—holding my hand while we waited to board and leaning against me on the plane. When we got home, I did the same thing I did in Kansas City. I helped her undress. I helped wash her—in the shower this time—and then I held her in bed. I knew that the shower had aroused her since she kept rubbing her thighs together as we snuggled in bed. But I also knew that letting me tend to her required more trust than letting me fuck her. And so I persevered. Even though we were both aware of my massive erection and her pained sighs.

It worked though, because the next day, a Tuesday, she asked if we could talk that night after she got home from work.

"Of course, lamb," I said. And then she came over of her own free will and kissed my cheek.

It was a start.

I didn't cook—I've never been interested in anything more complicated than grilled cheese—but I found a recipe online for bisque and did my best. Add in some wine and lightly burned dinner rolls, and it was a respectable meal, and I was rather proud of myself. When Poppy came home a few minutes later, I was just pulling my bisque splattered T-shirt over my head.

"Is it naked dinner?" she asked.

It was the most lighthearted thing I'd heard her say in almost two weeks.

"It can be if you want."

She smiled. "I do want."

We sat down and began eating, Poppy choosing hot chocolate over wine. The evening was clear, sprinkled with stars, and outside the snow-covered graves looked peaceful. Pretty even.

"So," Poppy began, looking down at her soup. "I'm not sure where to begin."

"Anywhere you like." I tried to pour every ounce of my loving her into my words. I wasn't sure where we'd gone wrong or how to fix it, but I wanted her to know what I was willing to do whatever it took.

She must have sensed this, because she looked up from her soup and met my eyes. "Okay."

I reached for her hand and squeezed it.

She took a deep breath and said, "I'm pregnant."

CHAPTER
TWELVE

"What?!"

I exploded out of my seat, practically tackling her. She let out peals of laughter as I picked her up and swung her around, burying my face in her neck.

Oh my God, I thought dizzily. *I'm going to be a father.*

A father.

To a baby.

My baby.

I spun her and spun her until we fell onto the couch with her on top of me, me making sure that her fall was gentle and safe. She raised up on her arms and looked down at me.

"I love you," I said and I meant it more than I ever had before.

"I love you," she said back with a huge grin. But then that grin faltered. "I know I've been…difficult these last two weeks. And I'm sorry. I am also sorry I didn't tell you sooner."

"You've known?" I didn't want to sound accusatory or make her feel badly, but this seemed like the kind of thing I should have known about seconds after she did.

She sighed and pushed herself back so that she was sitting in between my legs. "I found out the Monday before Thanksgiving. My period was a week late, and I remembered that I'd had the stomach flu the month before, and I thought maybe that had affected my birth control. So I took a drugstore test while I was at work and it was positive."

The Monday before Thanksgiving. The text message she'd sent me flashed through my mind.

Come home early tonight. I am excited to tell you about my day!

I thought she'd had a great day at work or something like that. Guilt crushed into me as I realized she'd been about to tell me that night. And then I'd been late.

"I wanted to tell you in person," she continued. "And I wanted it to be the right moment, you know? Just the two of us, here in our home. And then it kept not happening, and then I began to suspect that it would never happen. And then I began to think, 'Oh my God. If he isn't even around for me to tell him, how the hell is he going to be around to raise a child?'"

My eyes burned hot and I squeezed them shut. "Poppy…"

"And then the gala happened and you were late, and I

panicked. It wasn't even about the gala itself, it wasn't about the reason you were late, it was just about how I didn't know if I could trust you to help me with this. To be there for me."

The entire conversation replayed in my mind. "But Anton knew," I said quietly.

"Anton knew. He went down to the deli and bought me Sprites and ran interference for me while I napped in the office. He's been great."

I couldn't be angry about that. I couldn't be angry about Anton when the only one I had to blame was myself. But it still stung. It still scratched and scrabbled at the thin skin of my heart.

"But after Millie's funeral and your eulogy about knowing people and how sweet you've been to me this weekend, I realized something. That it wasn't you that made me scared. It was *me*."

I opened my eyes.

She rubbed self-consciously at her arms, hugging herself. "I'm scared, Tyler. I'm scared of being a mother. I'm scared of the baby taking time away from my foundation or my foundation taking time away from the baby. I'm scared of the baby changing us and the way we love each other." Her tears started falling, hard and fast now. "I mean, look at us! This baby has already changed us and hurt us! What if I've ruined everything by becoming pregnant?"

I sat up, crushing her to my chest. Her tears began to still as we sat together, her heartbeat slowly matching to mine. "Everything is going to change," I said. "And some of those changes are going to be hard. But there are going to be good things too, beautiful things, and I will be right here with you. I will be right here loving you and raising this child. And we will fuck up inevitably, with our child and with each other, but as long as we hold each other as close as God holds us to His heart, we will make it. I promise."

She sniffled. "Okay."

I kissed the top of her head, and we stayed there the rest of the night, cuddling and apologizing and promising and teasing, eventually stripping each other bare and sharing our joy the way we knew best.

"Are you Tyler Bell?"

I glanced over to the person standing next to me. I'd promised Poppy a peppermint steamer while we did the rest of our Christmas decorating together, and so I'd gone out to the local cafe to get one, not expecting to be recognized. I'd half-expected the person to be another Tylerette (sadly, the Hot Priest memes had not lost momentum after I left the clergy,) but it was an older Hispanic woman instead, possibly in her late fifties, with a sharply fashionable suit and leather laptop bag.

"I am Tyler," I answered warily. "How can I help?"

She smiled. "A friend of mine was on your dissertation board. He did me the favor of letting me read a copy. It was very, *very* impressive."

"Thank you," I said, still wary. Because this was weird.

"I have to ask, have you ever thought about publishing a book?"

I blinked. "No."

"I think your personal story is so compelling and raw. It would make an amazing memoir. But I also think that you have a gift for translating theology and religious history into something relatable, and that you should consider putting that work on a wider stage than just Princeton's house publisher. You could change a lot of lives, Mr. Bell, if you wanted to." She handed me her business card, which had *Maureen Reyes: Executive Editor* embossed in shiny black letters, and underneath it, the name of a very large New York publishing house.

I looked up at her, and she shouldered her bag with another smile. "Think about it. I'm happy to hear from you any time about any ideas you might have."

Holy shit, I thought after she left, turning the card over and over in my fingers, as if expecting it to vanish like leprechaun gold. *Holy shit.*

I got my coffee and Poppy's froufrou caffeine-free thing and headed out onto the snowy street, a giant grin stretching my face. I couldn't wait to tell Poppy; I mean, it was sudden and unexpected, but it made so much sense now that I thought about it. Writing something—a memoir or a book about modern theology or even church history—all of those options felt exciting and possible and *personal*. I wouldn't be able to hide behind anything if I wrote my memoir. Poppy would like that.

I rushed home, the cold world suddenly magical and alive and perfect, the holiday lights brighter and the garlands greener. I was having a baby and maybe I was going to publish a book and Poppy would be so excited and then I would be excited all over again and then we'd both think about the baby and get even more excited—on and on our happiness would loop, wider and stronger until we had no choice but to drop our decorating and go to the bed, where we'd spend the night making love.

I burst through the front door. "Poppy! Poppy! This crazy thing happened in the coffeeshop—"

I stopped. The miniature Christmas tree that we put on the kitchen table was half out of its box, tiny ornaments scattered on the floor around it. Her water bottle lay overturned on the table, water leaking slowly out of the open nozzle. Silence filled the townhouse, and I realized that the Christmas playlist had probably run out.

"Poppy?" I called, cautiously this time, my mind flashing to home intruders and serial killers. But then I stepped forward and saw the open door to our bedroom, and her kneeling by the bed. For a strange moment, I thought she might be praying...and then I heard the noise, the choked moan, and it was the same noise Morales had made in her office.

A pain noise.

A labor noise.

I set the drinks on the counter and jogged into the room, dropping to my knees next to her. "Lamb?" I asked, concerned, taking her hands in mine.

She looked up, her eyes distant and confused, her lips bloodless. "It hurts," she whispered. "I think...I think something's wrong with the baby."

Had I ever known what real fear was until this moment? Real pain? Every other experience in my life paled in comparison to this, sepia-toned facsimiles of terror bled dry of any real meaning, because now I knew what actual fear was. The way it dug its razored claws into your stomach and refused to let go, the way it pounded through your blood with that harsh, ceaseless neediness.

I'd only felt this way once before, when I'd gone into my parents' garage looking for batteries and instead saw my sister's feet suspended in the air. That horrible mixture of fear and helplessness galvanized by panic. I let it take me for one second, two seconds, three seconds; I let it hold me under and drown me.

And then I surfaced, squeezing her hands and using my other hand to smooth the hair away from her face.

"We have to go to the hospital," I said calmly, with the same confidence and possessiveness that I used with her in bed.

Her eyes cleared a little, finally focusing on me. "Okay,"

she replied weakly. "Will you take me?"

The pleading, childlike way she asked that broke my heart. "Oh, lamb." I gathered her into my arms and carefully embraced her. "I'm not leaving your side ever again."

She stiffened as another pain—could it be called a labor pain?—took her and I gentled her back and thighs and murmured reassurances and love into her ear until it passed.

"I'm going to get your insurance card and ID and then we'll go, okay, lamb?"

She nodded, as if she wasn't really hearing me, but I knew that she understood because she braced both hands on the bed and slowly got to her feet. I ran out to the kitchen and found her purse, rummaging through her wallet to find what we'd need, and then going back into the room for her. And what I saw ripped a hole right through me.

She stood with her legs slightly spread and her pants tugged down past her crotch. I could see the blood smeared across her thighs, glistening almost black on the fabric of her panties, but more horrifying was the expression on her face as she held her bloody fingers up to the light.

A blank expression.

An empty expression.

An achingly confused expression.

Blood. Blood is bad.

That terror came again, that panic, because something unspeakably awful was happening or about to happen and I was so helpless in the face of it. I started chanting the same mental prayer over and over again.

Please, Lord. Please no.

Please no.

Please no.

I knew my face must have looked the same as hers as I went to her, but I schooled my features with as much bravery as I could muster. I cleaned up the blood, found her new underwear and a pad, helped her pull on a fresh pair of pants. And then I picked her up and carried her to the truck, where she sat completely still and numb-looking while I raced us to the emergency room. Sometimes the pain would come and she would whimper, but that was the most she reacted to anything. Even when we made it to the triage room and the nurse started asking her questions, she answered in a dull, flat voice and mostly with one-word answers.

And I kept praying:

Please no.

Not this.

Please.

And then we were in the real ER room, Poppy clad in the hospital gown and hooked up to an IV, sipping a cup of water the nurses gave her to fill her bladder for the inevitable ultrasound. She said nothing, but every once and a while she would squirm and bury her face into the bed, her body stiff and arched with pain. Sometimes she curled into a ball, sometimes she doubled over, and towards the end, she got off the bed and started pacing, back and forth, back and forth.

Which was how the doctor found her when she entered. The doctor was a pretty woman in her thirties wearing a vivid blue dress and a gauzy patterned hijab, and the moment she walked in, she went right to Poppy and placed a soothing hand on her shoulder. Poppy stilled under her touch.

"I'm Dr. Khader," the doctor said. "I'm here to help you today."

She looked at Dr. Khader. "Okay," she said.

"I understand the nurses gave you a small dose of Tylenol to help with the pain. Do you feel like it's helped?"

Poppy's red lips pressed together and she swallowed, trying to muster her composure. "The pain still feels significant," she said. She managed this in steady, firm voice, the kind of voice she used discussing financial forecasts at work, and I realized how strong she was trying to appear, how in control. That was how Poppy liked to present herself to the world—collected and gathered and bulletproof.

Even when her entire world was bleeding out between her legs.

Dr. Khader nodded. "I thought so. Here's what we are going to do, Ms. Bell. We are going to do a quick examination and ultrasound to see exactly what's happening. Once we figure that out, we can more properly manage your pain. Do you have any questions or concerns before we get started?"

Poppy shook her head, still trying to be polite and put together, even though another pain was gripping her.

"Okay," Dr. Khader said. "I'm going to do a quick pelvic exam, followed by an ultrasound. May I help you onto the bed?"

Poppy nodded, white-faced, and Dr. Khader helped her settle on the bed, directed her how to position her legs. Dr. Khader spread a disposable sheet over Poppy's lap and pulled on a blue glove. "This will be uncomfortable," the doctor warned. "I will try to be as fast as I can."

The gloved hand went under the sheet while Dr. Khader's other hand pressed down on Poppy's abdomen from the outside.

I could tell the moment the examining began because Poppy sucked in a tight breath, closing her eyes. She was trying not to moan, I could tell, trying not to complain. Poppy had grown up in a world where emotions were pressed back, hidden behind a composed facade, and I could see how humiliating this was for her, this pain that kept breaking through the surface of her control.

"About eight weeks along," Dr. Khader murmured. "Which lines up with your last menstrual cycle." She pressed in a little deeper and Poppy gave out a little cry, and then Dr. Khader withdrew her hand, snapping off her gloves with practiced efficiency. "I'm so sorry that hurt." She seemed to mean it too, her dark eyes expressive with sympathy.

She reached for the ultrasound machine, pressing a few buttons and then squirting a blue gel on Poppy's stomach. She pressed the transducer into Poppy's skin, moving it around until the black and white static on the screen resolved itself. And then I could see it so clearly. I leaned forward, my heart crashing wildly against my ribs.

In the middle of the screen, there was a little gummy bear baby. A baby with a large head and small body, with short arms and legs. It looked exactly like the parenting ebook I'd downloaded onto my phone last night said a baby at eight weeks would look.

Except.

Except.

Please no.

Not this.

Please not this.

I'll do anything.

The gummy bear baby wasn't moving. At all. And then Dr. Khader clicked a couple buttons and a heart rate monitor appeared at the bottom of the screen.

Nothing.

No heartbeats.

No.

NO.

How could you, Lord?

How could *You?*

Dr. Khader kept looking and kept searching, but after a couple minutes, she pulled the transducer off Poppy's stomach. "I'm so sorry," she said gently. "But it appears that the baby has passed away."

Poppy's lips closed and her chin trembled, but she said nothing.

"Your cervix is partially dilated, which means your body is responding to the baby's death by attempting to expel the pregnancy. This is because you are at risk for infection if the pregnancy is not passed from your body." Dr. Khader put a hand over Poppy's. "Do you have any questions about what I've just said?"

Poppy took in a deep breath, moving her eyes to the ultrasound screen, which was now completely blank now that the transducer was put away. "What happens next?" she asked.

My stomach pitched at the sound of her voice—flat, businesslike. Her face more blank than the ultrasound screen. *You don't have to stay strong right now*, I wanted to tell her. *It's okay to be weak. It's okay to cry.*

Jesus knew that I was about to.

But Dr. Khader took Poppy's cold demeanor in stride. "Well, we can do one of three things. I can send you home with instructions to go see your obstetrician in a few days. You can let your body proceed naturally with the miscarriage, and be at home. Or I can give you some medicine that will speed the process along. We can either send you home for that, or depending on how quickly your body responds, you can be admitted to the hospital. Or, the final option is surgery—a procedure called a dilation and curettage. We will put you under general anesthesia, dilate your cervix and use a device called a curette to clear the uterine tissue, which usually takes less than thirty minutes. We'll monitor you afterwards for a few hours, and then you can go home." She squeezed Poppy's hand. "I know that was a lot of options at once, but I can give you two time and privacy to talk them over."

Poppy glanced over at me, her hazel eyes wide. Beneath the veneer of strength, I could see the fear and grief pooling inside of her, pressing up against the inside of her shell. Enough pressure and she would crack.

I just prayed she wouldn't break to pieces when it happened.

I will be there to pick them up, lamb, I silently promised her. But what I said out loud was, "I want this to be the easiest it can possibly be for you. What do you need, lamb?"

She closed her eyes and kept them closed while she addressed the doctor. "What is the way it will be over the fastest?"

"The surgery," Dr. Khader answered. "It does have some risks, however."

Poppy opened her eyes, and they were once again blank.

Empty. "I don't care," she said in a hollow voice. "Just make it be over. Make it stop hurting."

"We can do that," the doctor said. "And in the meantime, we will get you some real pain medicine. I'm going to go out and start the process and then I will be back in to discuss the specific risks with you."

She gave Poppy's hand one last pat and then left, the door closing behind her.

"Tyler?" Poppy asked, sounding tired.

"Anything, lamb. Anything you want. Just name it."

"Hold me?" Her voice cracked on the question, and that was what finally cracked me. I climbed up on the narrow bed and pulled her into my arm, letting my tears fall into her hair as she lay motionless against me, a numb, unfeeling doll.

CHAPTER THIRTEEN

It had been two weeks since the surgery. Two weeks since our short-lived joy had disappeared in a haze of blood and pain. I had been a father. Now I wasn't anymore. The feeling was surreal and vacating, like movers had come in the night and relocated all of my emotions and my perceptions, and had left me with nothing instead.

It was how I felt after Millie's death, but on steroids. Times a thousand. In fact, the only other time I remember feeling this gutted was after Lizzy's death. And this time it came pre-loaded with something else. Something extra.

Guilt.

Because this was my punishment. How could it not be? How could I have ever thought that a wife, a family, would be things I could have after what I'd done? After the calling I'd abandoned?

No. God was punishing me. Like Bathsheba and David's

infant after David had Uriah murdered, God had taken my child as payment for my sins. I deserved this pain, I supposed. I'd earned it with every sigh and moan and rustle of the sheets, and since I'd been so resolutely unrepentant, God had exacted his pound of flesh another way. With ounces of blood and a blighted joy. With just one black and white glimpse of the gummy bear baby that would never be part of our lives.

But why did Poppy have to suffer too? My prayers swung wildly from anger to bargaining to pleading and back to angry again.

Please.

Please not this.

Why this?

How fucking dare You?

How fucking could You?

My wife had become a woman I barely recognized. She took time away from work. She stopped reading, she stopped listening to Christmas music, and she sat by the window staring at the graveyard for hours. I could barely coax her to bed at night and into the shower in the mornings. Even though the semester was finished and I could stay home with her all day, it wasn't at all like we were in the same house together. Her mind—her soul—was somewhere else, wandering through the snowy cemetery maybe or reliving the same terrible memories in that linoleum-floored hospital room.

Please.

Please not this.

Please don't take my lamb's sparkle and spirit too.

I can't lose her. I can't.

I realized that in Kansas City, I had washed her and cradled her in order to win her trust. Now I had to do all of those same things simply to connect her to reality.

That spiral again. The same steps but with different meanings. The same actions but with different consequences. Maybe it was my penance, my duty, but I didn't care for her out of guilt—although the guilt hovered elsewhere. I cared for her because I loved her.

Poppy was depressed. Her doctor prescribed her medicine, and for once, the way she was raised helped—she had no stigmas about psychotropic drugs after growing up around rich women swilling Xanax and Ambien with their chardonnay.

A few more days passed. I made her move from the chair to the couch, which was closer to the fireplace, and I began reading books to her, finishing the mystery and moving on to *The Hitchhiker's Guide to the Galaxy* while I snuggled her on the couch. I heard her laughing at a couple parts, small little jerks of her ribs, and I kept reading as if I hadn't heard, feeling like a man who's encountered a wild animal in the woods. I didn't want to draw attention to the fact that she'd laughed, but *oh my fucking God*, she'd laughed. I hadn't realized how much I craved that sound until it had been gone from my life, and now here it was, creeping slowly around the edges of our home, crouching low by the fire to see if it was safe to come back.

At night, I crooned hymns low in her ears as she laid in my arms, the poor lamb shivering constantly even though we had quilts upon quilts piled upon us. I showered us together, washing her hair like a man might handle the world's finest painting. I got really good at making lobster bisque and not burning dinner rolls. I plied her with whiskey, which she rarely drank but liked to hold. I turned on Christmas music. I started reading the *Lord of the Rings* trilogy when *Hitchhiker's Guide* was finished.

And then, the Sunday before Christmas, something happened. She walked into the kitchen wearing a skirt and blouse, makeup freshly applied.

I, being used to our new hermit-like existence, was wearing a pair of boxer briefs and nothing else.

"I want to go to Mass," she said simply.

It was the first time she'd volunteered to leave the house of her own free will and for something other than a doctor's appointment.

I felt the wild animal wariness again. I didn't want to spook her with my open relief, my naked joy at seeing even this small stirring of life.

"Okay," I said evenly. "I'll get dressed."

Midnight Mass.

It started as a tradition in the Holy Land, where believers would gather in Bethlehem during the night and then, torches in hand, walk towards Jerusalem, making it to the city at dawn. A ritual that could fuse narrative into real life, where followers of Christ could stand in the same place He was born before making a pilgrimage to the Holy City.

It's changed over the millennia, morphed and warped into something different, but at its heart, it's the same. A re-enactment. A retelling. A redoing.

A liturgical creation of a new reality where Christ walks among us. At least, that's what Scholar Tyler would say about it.

In the few days since Poppy had left the house under her own steam, she'd gradually come more and more back to life. Singing along with Christmas carols. Yanking the book out of my hands when she felt like I was doing the voices badly. Even playfully pinching my butt in the kitchen.

Our own liturgy was slowly unfolding between the two of us. Glimpses of happiness and easiness and the divine. And like a Mass, I knew it couldn't be rushed, couldn't be pushed along. It had to unfold at its own pace, take its own time. So I held space for my lamb. And at the same time, I learned to hold space for my own grief and my own guilt. The idea that I'd earned our miscarriage as punishment haunted me, tormented me.

I read the annotations in my bible explaining that David

and Bathsheba's son probably died of natural causes, the act simply being ascribed to God's will as so many deaths were in those days. And I read David's own words in the Psalms:

As far as the east is from the west,
So far does he remove our transgressions from us.

But nothing helped.

I told you I was addicted to guilt. And like any addict, I needed to hit rock bottom. Which wasn't, as I thought, our miscarriage. It was the few minutes after midnight Mass, when I looked over and saw Poppy staring at the Nativity scene in front of us, the life-sized mannequins of the wise men and the Holy Family.

The life-sized baby Christ in the manger.

And then the Poppy-shaped shell she'd built around herself cracked, the raw emotion of the last month punching through her cocoon of numb self-control, and she started crying. No, not just crying.

Weeping.

The church was mostly empty now, which was good, because Poppy wept loudly, her hands over her face and her body hunched over so that her face was above her knees.

It cut at me to see my lamb like this, cut at me and also filled me with relief because I'd known this had to happen, I'd known that she needed to truly mourn. I wrapped an arm around her. "I'm here," I whispered quietly. "I'm here."

She said something into her hands, something so choked and teary that I couldn't make it out, and so I leaned closer and she said it again. "It's all my fault."

Four little words. Four dangerous, gangrenous, little words. Four words that—if you let them take root—would rot you away from the inside, would eat your soul and set decay festering in your heart.

I—Tyler Bell, former priest—should know.

"No, no, no," I begged her. "Don't say that. Tell me you don't believe that."

She raised her face to mine, her eyes wet and her cheeks splotchy. "It is my fault, Tyler. I didn't know if I wanted the baby! I said all of those terrible things about the baby changing my life, and what if God took the baby away because I didn't love it right away? Or what if God was saving the baby from me being a horrible mother?"

Jesus Christ, I thought, and the thought was half instinctive swearing and also half prayer. Is this what my own thoughts sounded like? Is this how dark and lost I was as well? When it came from my beautiful lamb, I could see how poisonous the guilt and shame were. How pointless.

And suddenly I took a step forward on my path, advanced along my spiral several paces. Quitting my addiction to guilt wouldn't be easy. It would probably be an emotional project for the next few years…maybe for the rest of my life. But I couldn't help Poppy leave her guilt behind if I didn't do the same with my own.

So I took a deep breath, held my crying wife close, and…let it go. Loosened my hold and dropped it to the ground. No more guilt for me. And no more for her.

"This isn't punishment, Poppy," I told her, with every ounce of certainty and love I could muster. "It's a tragedy and it's hard and it's sad, but God doesn't send pain to punish us or test us. Pain happens. Death happens. How we grieve and cope—that's up to us. Of course you were nervous about having a baby. Of course you were ambivalent. We would never punish a bride for feeling ambivalent before her wedding, or a man for feeling uncertain on the first day of a new job, so you can't punish yourself for how you felt about a child."

"But it took me so long to be happy about the pregnancy."

"Being unhappy or doubtful isn't a sin."

No more than leaving the priesthood. The thought came from somewhere outside of me, a beam of light illuminating the darkest corners of my soul. And for the first time in a year, I felt it. The shimmering, air-crackling feeling of God nearby. I only wished I could take that feeling and wrap it around Poppy like a blanket.

"I chose this religion," she said, hugging herself. "I chose this religion where everyone has these huge families, where it feels like having a baby is the most important thing a woman can do. And what does it mean for me as a woman if I can't do this one thing? What does it mean for me as a *Catholic* woman?"

I winced. "Poppy, no one would ever think you were

'less than' because you—"

"Because I had a miscarriage? Because I may not be able to carry a child? Look at the Bible, Tyler. Where are the godly infertile women in there?"

"Well, Sarah—"

"Ends up having a baby," Poppy interrupted. "Same with Rebecca and Rachel and Hannah. Every infertile woman in the Bible is eventually able to give birth. What does it mean if I never can? Does it mean that I'm not blessed or righteous? That there's something wrong with my soul as well as my body?" Her voice cracked on the last word.

I took a minute to answer, because I was near tears myself seeing her so devastated and also because I was still working through my new understanding of my guilt and how it had colored the way I'd read the scriptures for so long.

"The Bible was written in a very specific time and place, for a very specific culture," I explained. "I think that in the biblical environment having a child was the ultimate sign of God's grace and blessing. That Sarah ends up having a baby is the Bible's way of showing God's love and care for her— not God redeeming her through her womb, but through his love. That love can take any form. For the ancient Canaanites, it was children, but for us, it could be something completely different."

I gestured around the church, at the altar and at the

crucifix and at the tabernacle. "All of this—the lengthy bible readings and the liturgical rigmarole and the Eucharist—what do you think it's here for, lamb?"

She blinked, shaking her head. "I don't know."

"It's to remind us of our shared humanity. Of our quest to do better. And most importantly, of the fact that God loves us and helps us during that quest. Let Him love and help you now. Let Him give you grace."

The shimmering God-feeling intensified, and Poppy lifted her face to the crucifix. She tilted her head, as if listening to something only she could hear.

The bright overhead lights came on and a vacuum started running somewhere in the distance. The smell of smoke indicated the snuffing of candles in preparation for closing the church for the night, and still we didn't move.

Finally Poppy turned to me and said, "Okay. I will."

And then, holding hands and with tears still drying on our faces, we walked out into the biting cold of early, early, early Christmas morning. Up ahead the stars winked, like the Star of Bethlehem, and somewhere a baby was being born.

Maybe one day it would be ours.

But one hour into Christmas morning, a new beginning was being born for Poppy and me, and for now, that was enough.

EPILOGUE

POPPY
ONE YEAR LATER

Three a.m. Christmas morning. You have me sitting at the edge of a pew, my hands folded in my lap. *I wanted this*, I remind myself. *I asked for this.* But still, I'm nervous. Nervous that we'll get caught certainly, (although it's Jordan's church and I know he won't be back inside until dawn.) And I'm nervous about *why*–why we are acting out this fantasy or memory or whatever it is. It makes me nervous how much I want it, how much I dream about it. And it makes me nervous how aroused I am right now, doing nothing more than waiting for you in a dark, empty church.

When you asked me what I wanted for Christmas, I'm sure this wasn't what you expected to hear.

Your footsteps echo throughout the lofty sanctuary, loud and clear in the silence, and then I feel it, the gentle tap of two fingers on my shoulder, and I look up.

I practically come just by looking at you.

The flickering glow of candles illuminates your cheekbones, your square jaw, your nose that's bumped slightly in the middle from the time your brother pushed you face-first off a trampoline. Your face is scruffed with a day-old beard, and your hair has grown a little longer than you usually wear it, just long enough for me to slip my fingers through and grab onto. A small smile is on your wide mouth, just a hint of that dimple I love so much, and as always, you're so hot and intensely fuckable that I have to restrain myself from diving for your dick.

But it's what you're wearing that sets me off: belted black pants, long-sleeved black shirt, and— God help me—your collar.

Your collar, snowy white against the black of your shirt and setting off the strong lines of your throat. Your collar, which looks so natural on you, as if you'd never stopped wearing it. As if you were born to wear it. Did you know that you walk differently with that collar on? Stand differently? As if you're bearing both a burden and a joy at the same time. It's fascinating and beautiful and so fucking magnetic.

"I'm Father Bell," you say, as if we're meeting for the first time. "What brings you to the church today?"

Role-play. We haven't done it very often, so even though my heart is already racing and my thighs are already squeezing together at the sight of you in your collar, I feel a little self-conscious when I say, "I've never really been in a church before. I guess I'm just looking for guidance."

We're play-acting a version of how we first met. Me, lost and vulnerable, wandering into a church. You, intelligent and friendly and trying not to notice how your body responds to me.

You sit down on the pew, keeping two careful feet between us. For propriety. For morality. If this had been five years ago, I would have looked down, abashed at my own desire for you. I would have tilted my body away, trying to preserve your vows as I battled off the strongest attraction I'd ever felt in my life. But five years ago, we were in a church to pray.

Tonight, we are here to play.

I slide closer to you, making a show of adjusting my skirt so that you can see the top of my stocking and the clip of my garter belt. Your breath catches and our gazes meet momentarily. Then you blink away and clear your throat. "I'm happy to give any guidance you might like."

"And company too?" I let my hand drift over yours for the barest second before pulling it away. "I'm so lonely."

"Your loneliness can be cured through worship. And discipline." Your voice goes dangerous on that last word, and I shiver.

"Discipline?" I say in my breathiest voice, the one I know drives you mad.

"Spiritual discipline," you clarify sternly.

I unfasten the top two buttons of my sheer white blouse, reaching past the expensive fabric to run my fingers along my neck. You watch those fingers with intensity, swallowing as I dip my fingers lower to trace along the lacy edges of my bra. I let my legs uncross and begin to fall open…

"*Enough*," you say, truly stern now, those green eyes flashing. "Do you think it's acceptable to tempt a man of God? To torment him?"

Torment him, torment him.

The words reverberate throughout the room, furious echoes coming back to rebuke me. Searing rage rolls off you in waves and you abruptly stand, the outline of that delicious cock straining against your pants. You grab my wrist and yank me roughly to my feet, dragging me away from the pew and into the wide center aisle, where you throw me onto my knees.

This is part of it, I know, a part we had discussed and set boundaries for. But your anger feels so real right now, and my blood is pounding with equal parts adrenaline and lust, and I can't help but wonder if this fury you're summoning comes from a real place, real memories. Did you feel like I was some sort of Jezebel come to torment you back when we first met? I often felt like I was, and sometimes I still feel like that. But as you've told me, where there's guilt, there's grace, and right now my grace is fisting a hand in my hair and forcing me to look up.

I smile—I can't help it. You're so fucking handsome

and strong right now, so forbidden in that collar, and I love that you're mine. I love it so damn much that it's hard to breathe sometimes.

You frown at my smile. Your face is kinglike, displeased and radiating with power, and your pulse jumps on the side of your throat. "Is this amusing to you?" you demand, pulling my hair harder.

I wince but my smile recovers. I can't help it, really. "I'm just happy," I confess.

For a moment, your authoritative veneer thins and the sweet, tender man inside shines through it like a light. I know what I said has nestled itself against your heart. You give me an almost imperceptible wink followed by a swift grin, and then you're back to business, back to your role as my personal sex apostle. "Are you happy to be on your knees?" you growl.

I nod, licking my lips.

You growl again, this time without words, the hand not in my hair reaching for your belt buckle. With a few deft moves, your buckle and zipper are open and your fly is parted. Now my mouth really is watering, and you tease me, drawing out your cock but at first only tracing the tip along my lips, rubbing the underside of your shaft on my face. "Open," you say, and I do. You shove in rough and hard, and I moan at the silky feel of your skin, the way my tongue can trace the wandering paths of your veins.

"You're enjoying this," you accuse. "*Slut.*"

Oh God. My panties. So wet at that one terrible word.

You withdraw, your cock jutting up wet and dark from your pants. "What to do with a bad girl who enjoys her punishments, hmm? I could fuck your mouth, but I already know you like that too much. I could fuck your cunt, but a whore like you would get off on that, wouldn't she?"

Slut. Bad girl. Whore.

Awful words. Disrespectful words. But when the man I love calls me these things in private, my body responds enthusiastically.

You squat and reach under my skirt, impatiently nudging my knees farther apart with your hand. And then a finger is there, pushing aside my soaked panties and probing up. I gasp.

"So wet," you say, disgusted. You add another finger, your thumb working on my clit, and I can feel how slippery my pussy is, how it's making your skin slippery too. You know what you're doing as you crook your fingers and press into my secret spot, but you still glare at me as my cunt clenches around your fingers and as I ride out the waves on your hand. Your dick is practically carved from granite right now, stone hard and darker than the rest of you. I can see beads of pre-cum leaking from the tip. I want to lick them.

You notice where my eyes are going. "No. You can't have it."

It's hard to manage a pout while my body is still coming down from climax, but I do it, and I see the ghost of a smirk on your lips before you regain control. You stand up and grab my elbows, forcing me to my feet as well.

"It's time to confess your sins, little one," you say ominously. And then we're going toward the confessional.

This is the most pre-meditated part of our night together–lube, baby wipes and a towel are tucked under the confessional bench–yet I find myself completely lost in the moment as you drag me to the small wooden stall.

You sit, still keeping hold of me, and then you spin me so that I'm facing away from you. My skirt is pulled down and my panties torn off (I've learned to buy cheap ones when I know I'll be fucking you.) The garters and stockings stay.

"Take off your blouse." The slight hoarseness in your voice betrays you. I feel your hands roughly plumping and squeezing my ass as I do what you ask. "Now kick off your heels."

I obey and then I look back at you over my shoulder.

You're sitting with your legs spread and your feet flat on the floor, your pants lowered just enough for your cock to be free. Your jaw is set, your eyes are dark, and your hands are rough on my skin as you continue to fondle my ass.

You own this confessional. You own me.

I see you reach over for the small white tube, clicking it open and lazily dribbling the cold, clear gel onto your cock. The first time we did this, we used anointing oil, too desperate for each other to wait to find something more suitable. (Or at least something less blasphemous.) The memory makes my core heat up all over again, everything below my navel tingling and humming and alive.

"You're making me sin," you reprimand as your hand begins to slowly pump your cock. Lube glistens over the dark, hot skin, and I see you curl your fist tighter. "You're making me do something I shouldn't do. You're making me want it. That's very, very bad of you."

Can a man look regal as he strokes himself? I don't know, but that's how you look right now, with the muscles of your arms and shoulders bunching beneath your shirt and your powerful legs splayed out and your magnificent cock so prominent and proud.

"Am I in trouble?" I ask coyly, batting my eyelashes.

"So much trouble," you mutter and then one of your hands wraps around my waist and yanks me back and down.

The moment your dick presses between my cheeks, I feel my nervousness from earlier melt away. *This* is what we do, *this* is who we are. I can't lie and tell you that you being a priest didn't make me want you at first. I can't lie and tell you that the forbidden beginning to our relationship doesn't still get me hot, get me off sometimes when I think about it.

But at the heart of us, at the bedrock of our love,

there is only raw trust and deeply rooted hope. Yes, I fell for you because you were a priest. But I stayed in love with you because you were you, Tyler Bell, smart and jealous and spacey, and devoted and tortured.

All of this I feel as the wide crest of your crown slowly pushes past the first ring of muscle and then the second, all while you are pressing me down onto you, impaling my tight ass on your erection. I focus on breathing and opening, on relaxing for you, breathing in controlled, shuddering breaths until my ass cheeks are pressed into your groin and I'm as far down as I can go. You've bottomed out, and you allow yourself a muttered *fuck, that's tight.*

We pause like this, you leaning your forehead against my back and me speared on your cock, facing away from you and looking out of the open door of the confessional and into the empty sanctuary.

"Ready, lamb?" you whisper in my ear.

I hate not being able to see you, but it forces me to pay attention to everything else even more: the rasp of your voice, the rough pads of your fingers as they caress my breasts, the thick erection filling me up so full that I can barely stand it.

And then there's no telling where the role-play ends and we begin anymore, because your hands move to my waist, lifting me up and down, up and down, and it's rough enough that my safe word floats to the surface of my mind. But for every deep thrust where you bury yourself to the balls, for every whispered *slut* and *make me come, make me fucking come*, there is a light kiss between my shoulder blades, a hand reaching up to tuck a strand of hair behind my ear.

I love it. And by the end of it, the emotional charge of our play-acting and the sweetness lingering underneath and the brutal ass-fucking have all contributed to my mind feeling blissed out, spaced out, my orgasm erupting out of nothing and rippling through nothing, and I'm a body of contradictions—tense and relaxed, shuddering but calm, present but also soaring far above it all.

As I come, you move my ass onto your dick so hard and fast that I almost scream, and then you grunt *lamb*, and finally, you pulse deep and long inside of me, marking me as yours as you release, your fingers digging into my waist.

Te amo, you croon into my hair as we both come down. *Te amo.*

I love you.

"I love you too," I mumble, my body too come-drunk to operate properly.

You chuckle at the way I'm slumped back against you, and then you're helping me up, helping me clean myself before you help me dress again.

We are both sheepish as teenagers when we emerge from the confessional and into the sanctuary. You even have an adorable blush high in your cheeks as you pluck unconsciously at your collar. We will drive back to our hotel and then wake up in a few hours to spend Christmas with your parents. But first…

"That was the best Christmas present I've ever gotten," I tell you, leaning up on my tiptoes to kiss your mouth. "Now can I give you yours?"

"Of course," you say, amused and happy, and I skip off to my purse where I pull out the small box. As I hand it to you, I think about this year. About what we've lost, but also what we've gained. My flagship studio exceeding all expectations. The book deal for your memoir, which already has huge buzz a few months before it hits the shelves. A new place in the city. A better understanding of each other.

You tug the ribbon of the box and then carefully open the wrapping paper by sliding a finger under the seams. And when you see what's inside the narrow box, tears fill your eyes.

"I don't know what's going to happen," I tell you. "I'm scared. But I know that no matter what happens, we will endure it together."

"Oh my God, lamb," you breathe in wonder. The box tumbles to the ground as you reach for my face. And before your mouth crashes into mine in the happiest, sweetest kiss I've ever had, I catch sight of your present upturned on the ground.

A white stick with a little blue cross in the window. The answer to a hundred thousand prayers. Prayers that seem to swirl and dance around me now as you rejoice with me.

"Amen," I murmur to those prayers, my lips moving against yours as I speak the word out loud. "Amen."

Afterword

I wasn't sure how to end this book. Romance wisdom seemed to dictate that there are two kinds of Happily Ever Afters: marriage and having children. If Book One ends with a marriage, then Book Two should end with a baby. It makes sense and also, who doesn't love babies? More importantly, who doesn't love reading about a romantic hero melting over his baby?

Part of me wanted to end it with a happy, healthy baby, but as someone who's suffered through three miscarriages, I also resented the idea that Tyler and Poppy's narrative would need to be "redeemed" with a healthy birth. I didn't like that we so rarely have a place in romance for women who struggle with infertility, who may never have the Happily Ever After that our culture teaches us we need to have. Not to mention the women and couples who consciously choose to remain childless. Two people can have a fulfilling and deep life together no matter how many places they set at the dinner table.

So instead, I ended the story with a possibility. With a hope. I reserve the right (as the capricious author I am) to decide for sure what happens to Tyler and Poppy after this curtain closes, but for now, we end with the knowledge that whatever happens, Father Bell and his lamb will still live happily (and sexily) ever after.

Want More Provocative Romance?
Meet Father Bell's brother Sean…
An Entertainment Weekly Top 10 Romance of 2018!

I'm not a good man, and I've never pretended to be. I don't believe in goodness or God or any happy ending that isn't paid for in advance. In fact, I've got my own personal holy trinity: in the name of money, sex, and Macallan 18, amen.

So when the gorgeous, brilliant Zenny Iverson asks me to teach her about sex, I want to say yes, I really do. Unfortunately, there are several reasons to say no—reasons that even a very bad man like myself can't ignore.

1. She's my best friend's little sister.
2. She's too young for me. Like *way* too young.
3. She's a nun. Or about to be anyway.

But I want her. I want her even with my best friend and God in the way, I want to teach her and touch her and love her, and I know that makes me something much worse than a very bad man. It makes me a sinner.

And it's those very sins that are about to save me...

Sinner is available on all vendors now!

ALSO BY
SIERRA SIMONE

Co-Written with Julie Murphy:
A Merry Little Meet Cute (A holiday raunch-com)

The Priest Series:
Priest
Midnight Mass: A Priest Novella
Sinner
Saint

Thornchapel:
A Lesson in Thorns
Feast of Sparks
Harvest of Sighs
Door of Bruises

Misadventures:
Misadventures with a Professor
Misadventures of a Curvy Girl
Misadventures in Blue

The New Camelot Trilogy:
American Queen
American Prince
American King
The Moon (Merlin's Novella)
American Squire (A Thornchapel and New Camelot Crossover)

Co-Written with Laurelin Paige

Porn Star

Hot Cop

The Markham Hall Series:

The Awakening of Ivy Leavold

The Education of Ivy Leavold

The Punishment of Ivy Leavold

The London Lovers:

The Seduction of Molly O'Flaherty

The Wedding of Molly O'Flaherty

ABOUT THE
AUTHOR

Sierra Simone is a USA Today bestselling former librarian who spent too much time reading romance novels at the information desk. She lives with her husband and family in Kansas City.

Sign up for her newsletter to be notified of releases, books going on sale, events, and other news!
www.thesierrasimone.com
thesierrasimone@gmail.com

CPSIA information can be obtained
at www.ICGtesting.com
Printed in the USA
LVHW040957240722
724214LV00006B/208